RIEMANN ZETA

RIEMANN ZETA:

ZERO SUM

NICHOLAS B. BEESON

iUniverse, Inc.
Bloomington

Riemann Zeta
Zero Sum

This is a work of fiction. All of the characters, names, incidents, organizations, and dialogue in this novel are either the products of the author's imagination or are used fictitiously.

iUniverse books may be ordered through booksellers or by contacting:

iUniverse
1663 Liberty Drive
Bloomington, IN 47403
www.iuniverse.com
1-800-Authors (1-800-288-4677)

Because of the dynamic nature of the Internet, any web addresses or links contained in this book may have changed since publication and may no longer be valid. The views expressed in this work are solely those of the author and do not necessarily reflect the views of the publisher, and the publisher hereby disclaims any responsibility for them.

Any people depicted in stock imagery provided by Thinkstock are models, and such images are being used for illustrative purposes only.

Certain stock imagery © Thinkstock.

ISBN: 978-1-4620-6034-4 (sc)
ISBN: 978-1-4620-6036-8 (e)
ISBN: 978-1-4620-6035-1 (dj)

Library of Congress Control Number: 2011918456

Printed in the United States of America

iUniverse rev. date: 11/29/2011

Thanks to:

Becky Carlton, who put up with my craziness; she is an amazing person and friend.

Harrison, whose light heart helped me find a way to keep going when I was stuck. ("You want to know what is going on in my head?" *Well yeah!* "You're an idiot.")

My parents, who always saw me as better than I saw myself to be. (Mom, thank you for taking the phone calls and saving me from my dumb mistake. Dad, you made my work even better and made *me* even better.)

Vanessa Brenard, who came into my life just in time to give me such a beautiful cover. (Thank you, **Blaise**, for finding her.)

Doug and **Victoria**, for being supportive siblings, even when I am a pain.

Amy Chapin, for being a great teacher, mentor, and friend.

Amy Sigler, **Jamie** Collyer, **Stephen** Block, and all of my other friends who have been supportive and helpful throughout this process.

INTRODUCTION:

In *Riemann Zeta: Zero Sum,* the pronouns *they, them,* and *their* are used as singular pronouns for the two main characters. The obscuration of their sex is intentional. This element of design encourages the reader to imprint his or her own experiences upon the characters and to connect to the story.

THE FIRST RAYS OF a sudden desert dawn shatter the crisp, chill air of the pervasive night. As the sun heats up the arid road, a lone vehicle pushes on in much haste.

The driver travels with nothing but a few articles of clothing in the trunk and with orders for the new job, in a new city—*to start anew.*

The driver wishes for something to listen to other than the hum of the overworked engine. *That would be a godsend.* Absently, the driver tries the radio and still gets nothing but static.

The vehicle's computer system suddenly picks up a service station announcement and interrupts the mundane drone of the engine. "Stop and be refreshed at our station! Get coffee! Use the bathroom! Or just get out and stretch! This is the last station for the next three hundred miles, so you may wish to stop!"

The annoying musical accompaniment, sounding more like breaking glass than music, belies the truth of the announcement. Recognizing the accuracy of the distance, the driver slows down to stop.

Upon opening the door, the recorded voice that was used for the announcement declares, "Welcome to our store! Thank you for stopping here!"

Vision adjusting to the white fuzzy light in the store, the driver squints and focuses on the restroom, hesitating only to check out what the clerk is doing. The young man is barely into his early twenties; his hair is a blond mop of good length, and his clothing looks slept in. *No more than a day, maybe two*, notes the driver about the clothing, expertly judging the depth of the wrinkles and the number of food smears decorating the outfit. The clerk is making lines of cocaine on the glass part of the counter. Unimpressed, the driver continues on to the restrooms.

Opening the door to the restroom releases a vile stench that immediately stings the eyes and instantly makes anyone feel dirty. To call this a restroom would be a farce. *Animals don't even leave a mess like this.* With breath held, the driver moves quickly, closing the door to get out of the shit hole and away from this horrible room.

Eyes stinging, the driver hears the clerk call out, "Are you okay?" Tossing the driver some wet wipes, the clerk continues without much concern, "Here, clean up with these." Beyond the watery eyes, the driver notices that this young man is missing his left ring finger at its base.

"Sorry for the mess; the scrubbers aren't working," the clerk apologizes, as someone else behind the counter joins him.

A good six inches taller, this other male is a contradiction in style to the first clerk. The most notable thing about the new associate is his black hair, styled in a complicated and time-consuming way. Starting as short-trimmed hair at the point of his chin and moving up the left side of his face into his hairline, his hair then continues around the back and upper parts of his head and ends at the right upper area of the forehead. The other parts of his head are shaved clean, even his left eyebrow. This swirl of hair grows ever longer the closer it gets to his forehead. His clothing is similar to the other clerk's, minus the creases and the stains.

Probably the first time he has ever worn them, the driver guesses. The driver makes a move to the refrigerator cases to get something cold to drink. On the way to the counter, the driver reads "Rick"—just Rick—on the first clerk's shirt.

His second confirms this: "Rick, do you have something to hit this with?" He points to the nowhere-near-straight lines of cocaine on the glass.

Rick reaches into his shirt pocket, fumbles around trying to pull out a fake cash bill, and says, "Yeah, Jeff; hold on. I just roll this and we'll hit it ... heh, it's my way of shirking it to the old order."

The driver stands awaiting service and counts twelve lines of coke. Each one is about a foot long. Rick takes a line, and Jeff takes one, too. Only after indulging does Rick look up and ask as well as he can, "Is that all?"

"Would you like some?" asks Jeff.

Saying nothing, the driver pulls out an M.E. (monetary electronic) card and flashes a badge in response to the offer.

Rick asks nonchalantly, "You going in or coming out?"

Swiping the M.E. card and grabbing the drink with one fluid motion, the driver walks out.

"Must be going in," Jeff says to no one in particular, but he assumes Rick is paying attention. Rick, already in an altered state, is only able to manage a nod.

The driver gets back into the vehicle and starts it. There is a "Thank You!" announcement in the same recorded voice as the vehicle leaves the service station, heading for a destination beyond the horizon.

I know every generation over time thinks how the new generation is full of losers or is wasting away the gift of youth. Like Jeff and Rick back there, getting messed up at work, 'cause it doesn't matter what they do, working in the middle of nowhere. Just as I have no idea what it is like to be waiting for something else to do with my time. This new job has the possibility to be full of moments like that. Hopefully the lax laws of the City will not leave me bored—just looking into who has stolen the paperclips from the office. Ha-ha. Paperclips.

The driver notices the emptiness of the road and accelerates. Passing low scrub and slowly waking desert creatures, the driver feels the hum of the vehicle becoming hypnotic. Outside the window, wisps of what look like dancing veils spin and twirl as the vehicle flashes by. The sun is high by now, but the cold of night is not yet willing to let go of the earth.

Check into new job.

Check into apartment.

Find closest node and set it up as primary. Hopefully there is access from my apartment building.

I hope I am not assigned a partner. That would only complicate things.

What will I do then? Still check into the new job and apartment—but setting up the closest node might not happen for a couple of days. That should be all right. The system should allow for a couple of days before I need to set it up. No more than a week.

After pressing on for some time, the vehicle notifies the driver of a radio station. Not too long after that, the city information guide comes on, asking, "Do you have a destination in mind?" The driver grabs the orders off the passenger seat and reads the name and address. The city guide then asks if the driver wishes for an autopilot or vocal and visual directions. The driver opts for the vocal and visual directions. The directions start when the driver reaches the City.

The City doesn't start with the small houses and low towers of old. The City just starts. The first two towers that the driver passes are the smallest anywhere in the City, only eighty-three stories above ground. The shapes and colors of this city's architecture are as varied as random spasms, from dark and brooding twisted knurls to expansive pastels and flamboyant neons. The variety is evidence of the City's collective creative minds.

As the buildings start, so does the traffic.

Traffic seems to be a problem that spans space and time. Which also happen to be the cause *of traffic: space and time.* This thought rolls around the driver's head while navigating in and out, up and down through the traffic.

The driver arrives at the intended destination, which happens to be near the center of the City. Taking the orders from the vehicle's audio directions, they enter the formidable building labeled Civil Central Command. The emptiness of the lobby greets the driver upon entering. There is nothing in this lobby. The floor is the only thing that isn't plain, with its large City crest inlaid in the middle. Contrary to perception, this space is extremely quiet, almost muffled. Even the greeter, the sole person in the lobby, is plain. Nothing about her seems exciting. The room and this woman seem to be in competition to be the most unremarkable. She suits the room.

As the driver moves across the lobby toward her, she moves forward in turn. They meet in the middle, on the City crest.

"Good day to you," she says with zest. From this central point the entire room can be observed. The odd part of this lobby is that there is nothing to break the blandness—no windows, doors, stairs, nothing—not even a place to sit.

"May I assist you on this fine day?" she asks. Her enthusiasm contradicts the blandness of her position.

The driver shows her the orders and points to the office listed on the top while continuing to scrutinize this environment.

Perusing the information, she says, "So, you are the one? I was told that you were to be arriving in another day or so."

Without waiting for a response, she motions for them to move to the back wall. Placing her hand on a seemingly random place on the wall, she activates lights behind the walls to shine through. At this point, the secrets cloaked by the plain room's drab façade are exposed.

Behind the walls, to the left and right of the door, are military grade weapons, all of them automated and trained on only the driver. She turns and looks up at the ceiling. The driver's eyes follow. The illusion of the flat ceiling is gone. In reality, the ceiling is a dome, with a man sitting in a turret controlling the weapons. Without either one saying a word to the other, the greeter and the turret operator exchange significant looks as part of security protocol. A doorway opens behind the greeter.

She hands back the orders and says kindly, "Take this to the end of the hall and make a left. Then go to the twenty-third floor. The second door on your right is where you need to go. Ben should be there to meet you. All right?"

She smiles and steps back, away from the door, allowing it to close between them. As the door locks back into place, the lobby returns to its plain, dull state. The driver watches her for a moment, as she still faces the door, smiling. She finally turns away from the door once the driver moves down the hall.

At the far end of the hall, people can be seen passing by. The driver makes a left at the end and finds that the hall goes on for some time. There are very few doors in the hall, and every so often someone enters the hall from these doors; all give some form of greeting to the driver. Making it to the lift, the driver gets on alone.

The smooth, quiet ride to the twenty-third floor seems to take no time at all. Exiting, the driver finds that there are only four doors in this hall. Walking in the second door, the driver expects to be met by Ben but finds no one. The room beyond the door is a small waiting room decorated in an old-fashioned Art Deco style. The driver muses that the decorator's intent was something from the twentieth century. The anteroom is lit with harsh fluorescent lighting; the floors are covered with bad carpeting, nondescript but ugly. The magazine rack has genuine antique magazines or possibly really good knockoffs; it is hard to tell with a cursory scan. The bell sitting on the counter completes the look.

A sharp ring of the bell accomplishes its job; a man comes flying out of the back room.

"What are you doing?" he rebukes the driver. "The bell is only for show; you can break it by hitting it that hard!"

This must be Ben, assumes the driver, at the same time doubting Ben's claims that the bell was abused.

Ben is a young man, about average height, with a solid look about him. He has brown hair and lightly tanned skin, but his eyes are something to behold—green, but more. Most eyes reflect light, but these seem to emit it. The green is so brilliant that the driver wonders if they have been altered.

Ben quickly recovers from his swift accusation. "I'm sorry about that. It's just that I have worked so hard to save up and get this," he says while holding the bell and carefully polishing off the fingerprints. Returning it to its rightful place on the counter, he finally declares, "I'm Ben; may I assist you?"

Silently, the driver hands him the orders, which Ben takes and starts to look over. Ben pauses, looks up, and is about to ask a question but decides against it. After reading the orders, he loads the information he needs into the mainframe.

"All right. Come with me, and we'll see the Cap," Ben says, leading the way to the back door.

The journey takes them down a couple of steps, into a pit area filled with a maze of desks, and then back up a couple of steps to a set of large double doors. The doors have the City crest on them but have no handles. The two stop a few paces away from the door. A second later the doors silently open inward.

Ben nods toward the entryway and points out matter-of-factly, "He's a nice guy; just don't piss him off."

Stepping forward into the office proper, the driver immediately starts cataloguing and making mental notes of its layout and contents. The office is a profound contrast to the last place the driver saw the City crest. This room has places to sit, a bookshelf with some antique books, two other doors in addition to the main door, a desk, and plants. Off to the right is a couch that has a small table in front of it and to the left is another bookshelf. It has six shelves and is about six feet long. Only the fourth shelf from the bottom has books on it; the other shelves have plants or personal things, such as awards and medals. The driver examines the plants, observing that two of the plants are native to desert environments: one is a desert rose in bloom, a white flower with a pinkish-red along the outside of each petal; and the other is a bird of paradise flower. There is also one *polystichum* fern and a bonsai plant. The final plant is unknown to the driver. It has smooth green leaves and a flower that crosses over itself. The flower to this unknown plant is red and looks like it is a fire sword. One of the other doors is to the right of the couch, and one is in the back left corner of the office. The desk is positioned in the center and toward the back. Standing behind it is a tall, silver-haired man.

"Come in," he says, his voice booming. His voice is not only deep, it's also a bit gravelly, which is unexpected from a man of his thin, fit stature. Using his hands as he speaks, he directs the driver to come toward the desk. The driver stops two paces behind a seat in front of the desk. As the driver approaches, the silver-haired man sits down and starts looking over a file from the copy that is now in the mainframe.

"I see here that you passed the driver test. You know that this is not a restricted city?" The Cap looks up only with his eyes at the driver, "You've never driven in anything like this before. Therefore, I've decided that you will have a partner, and I'm going to disregard this request for a solo assignment for the time being." The Cap leans back in his chair, running both his hands through his hair and locking his fingers behind his head. "I don't know if you requested that ... or if it was the Council trying to meddle." Cap says the last comment to himself. "Either way, I don't care; I'm turning it down."

The Cap pauses and looks the driver up and down to ascertain any reaction to his authority. He interprets the nearly imperceptible response as confusion. This is acceptable to the Cap, and so he starts his "new blood" speech by clearing his throat. It isn't a very long speech, not nearly long enough to cover all of the things that someone who just moved in should know, but it is enough for newcomers to get started working here. The oratory intends to instill a healthy level of respect in those working in the unrestricted city.

The Cap ends his briefing by asking if the driver has any questions. The driver shakes their head no, and the Cap then shows the driver out to where Ben is waiting. He instructs Ben to get the driver in-processed and set up with appropriate accommodations. Punctuating this order and expressing his confidence in Ben, the Cap pats Ben's arm just below the shoulder. Ben nods briskly in acknowledgment and begins the grueling task of in-processing.

The in-processing takes the better part of four hours. *Bureaucracy's reliable contribution to the simplest of tasks,* the driver thinks so often throughout the rest of the day that it becomes more of a mantra than an observation.

Finally, Ben gives the driver an address of a place to stay and says, "I don't understand it, but your orders have you staying on the low end of town. Most of the time I can change that, but I can't change yours. Sorry. Your partner will meet you at your place at 0800. Have a good night." By this time, the driver isn't paying much attention anymore, and they both wave good-bye as they head off in different directions to make their ways home.

With the day wasted, darkness has fallen by the time the driver finally makes it to the address Ben provided. Not surprisingly, it takes less to get into the apartment than it did to in-process at the Civil Central Command. Without looking at the accommodations, the driver lies down on the bed and falls asleep instantly as head meets pillow.

The moonlight accentuates the well-toned muscles of a figure on the cliffs rimming the desert. Each movement this figure makes up the cliff is quick and done with ease. Soon the figure is standing on the top of the cliffs, with a city's glow ahead and the cold, dark desert behind.

In the desert surrounding the city, all creatures, seen and unseen, are preparing for the building storm. As a sense of uneasiness vibrates across the desert floor, the moon, unfazed by the pending wrath of nature, continues to shine brilliantly.

The thunderclouds roll over the defiant moon, and the figure is washed in darkness. The darkness is welcomed as the rain comes down upon the dark figure. The rain drenches the dark figure's long black hair, which quickly turns even darker as the rain is absorbed. So, too, does the rain absorb into the clothing—or what used to be clothing. The dark figure takes a moment to embrace the rain with arms outstretched and enjoys the coolness as rivers run across their body.

After embracing the rain, the dark figure starts walking toward the light of the distant city. Some pieces of the tattered, threadbare clothing start to disintegrate under the weight of the rainwater as they move and essentially melt away one thread at a time. Removing the remnants that can't be saved, leaving just the bare essentials, the dark figure walks at a brisk pace.

The City quickly morphs from just a glowing light into a figure itself. Long, slender columns of light reach high into the night sky, almost able to touch the low-hanging storm clouds that are passing over. A large smile spreads across the dark figure's face—a smile that matches the well-toned, perfect body but is corrupted and menacing when coupled with the intensity and malice emanating from the dark figure.

In even less time than it took to reach the City from the cliffs, the dark figure enters the City and locates an apartment building. Walking in as if owning the building, the dark figure moves to the thirteenth floor and finds the corner apartment. One blow from the heel of the dark figure's right foot breaks the handle clean off with very little noise. A left pinky is all that is needed for the dark figure to bypass all of the security and unlatch the door. With no alarms, the dark figure slips in, unknown to all.

William Springer is a low-level chemist, and is not very good at his job. In spite of this, he thinks that he is getting somewhere in the company, since he is working on a prestigious project. He feels he'll get a promotion soon. He's even convincing himself that his beloved Dana will return. As he starts to fall asleep, he says aloud, "Then Dana will come back."

Dana has left William, because they wanted to start a family, and William failed to tell Dana of his involvement in a major chemical spill that effectively rendered him sterile. On the outside chance that he did father a child, the malignant chromosomal cocktail he would donate to any offspring would ensure his parenting opportunity would be short-lived. Multiple birth defects would doom any child he fathered within a year.

Knowledge comes in many forms, and for Dana it came eight months after the incident, in the form of a lunch with her friend Sara, who was the wife of the medical examiner. During this lunch, they started to talk about the challenges of raising a family in the City. The wandering conversation led Sara to tell Dana about a tragic incident, a chemical spill that had left a poor man who was trying to become a father effectively sterile. Sara was obviously unaware that Dana was the unfortunate woman married to William Springer. Dana calculated very quickly that she was married to the "poor man" and that she would never have a family if she stayed with him.

William had neglected to inform Dana of anything related to the spill. He said nothing of the danger to her health, particularly that the chemicals would remain in his body for almost a week and could hurt her if passed to her by the exchange of bodily fluids. This could render her sterile, or worse yet, dead. Before the nefarious chemicals cleared his system, the couple went on a romantic trip coinciding with the time they were trying to start their family. After Dana confirmed her fears and William's lies by omission, she left him.

Every night since she left, William has replayed this pageant in his head, searching for remedies. This night is no exception, and as these recollections roll through his head like waves intertwined with the darkness of sleep, William distinctly hears himself say out loud, "Dana will come back ..." His voice trails off as sleep overcomes him, pursuing thoughts known only to him.

Just over two months after Dana walked out, William awakens to hear the shower in his flat running. Half awake, he stumbles into the hallway toward the bathroom. As he starts to open the bathroom door, he becomes filled with joy when he inhales Dana's perfume wafting through the air. "Dana, you've come back!" William cries out enthusiastically. There is no response; he hesitantly steps into the steam-filled room. Stopping in front of the running shower, trying to see through the steam, and with sorrow in his voice, William attempts to lay bare his soul. "I am so sorry, dear—"

His words are cut short, not by choice—there is a lot more to say; after all, Dana has returned. William's brain tries to interpret all the data in front of him, but one fact keeps drawing his attention. Red.

Red? he thinks. *It's not her favorite color, and it doesn't match this room.* None of this makes any sense to William, and finally all he sees is red. His blood shoots out from the lacerated artery in his neck and covers everything in front of him.

William stands with his arms at his sides for a second more and then collapses, as all of the strength of his being spatters the room. Standing right behind William, holding a long, broken piece of glass that smells of Dana's perfume and drips blood off one edge, is the dark figure. Blood runs down the broken glass as if it is bleeding. Letting the glass fall to the floor and shatter, the dark figure steps into the running water to clean the wound from the shard and remove any residual of the one once known as William Springer.

The driver wakes up in a cold sweat from the dream when the intercom to the apartment buzzes. Simultaneously, the pager from Civil Central Command goes off. Unknown to the driver, both nuisances are from the driver's new partner. Neither seems to be a welcome addition to the driver's routine.

Rising out of bed and quickly preparing for the arrival of their impromptu guest, the driver takes quick stock of their new domicile. The first room entered and put to use is a bathroom attached to the bedroom. It's just large enough to comfortably fit the standard necessities. Emerging from the bathroom, the driver assesses and appreciates the size and configuration of the bedroom. The short hallway out of the room has closed doors on either side before it opens up into a casual living room that features a half wall separating the kitchen into its own space. Across the living room from the hall is the main doorway. The driver opens the door.

Standing in the doorway is a person facing the other way. The person is a few inches shorter than the driver and has long, black hair. The driver assumes that it is a woman because of the sound of her voice and her very nice hourglass figure. She is talking to someone, but no one is in front of her in the hall.

"No, Ben, I will not be there."

As the door opens to its fullest, she turns around quickly. As she turns, her hair glints its true color, which is a deep purple.

"Ben! I have to go now. Yes, I will pass along the information about the appointment and the other thing. Don't worry." Ben's insistence can be felt in her curt responses to his unheard interrogation. With a deep, audible sigh, she ends the call and bends down to grab a bag that has sweet smells emanating from it. She holds it up and says cheerfully, "I brought some breakfast."

The driver steps aside to invite her in. She walks in and starts straightaway to the kitchen.

"I didn't know what you like, so I got a little bit of everything."

"Thanks?! I don't know when the last time I ate was," the driver answers back, mostly to themself. Still standing in the doorway, slightly stunned by the smooth aggression of this visitor, the driver is trying to calculate why they aren't more alarmed. Maybe it is the lack of sleep, or maybe it is the speed and calmness of this intruder. The driver feels no imminent threat. Finally, collecting enough sense, the driver follows her into the kitchen, where she has laid out most of the food.

She stops and extends her hand, saying, "By the way, I'm Remmington, your partner, but you can just call me Remmie."

The driver takes her hand and shakes it.

"Can I give you some advice? You didn't know who I was—you shouldn't have let me in."

The driver offers a reply by silently removing a pistol and harness from under the back of their shirt and placing the items on an empty bookcase at the side of the room.

Chuckling, Remmington replies, "You might just make it in the City. I am going to guess that either you have been here before or someone told you about how the City is."

"Not exactly. I've never been here, and no one had to tell me about the City." The driver stretches out the fatigue from the previous day and considers that this is not the whole truth before continuing on with common knowledge about the City. "I understand that the City has the least amount of regulations in order to develop the best in technological advancements. This lack of regulation can lead to a rise in some types of crime."

"That's a nice way of putting it. 'Some types' is right on. One week, some of these people are on top of the world, with the latest and greatest idea. The week after that, they are no one and have nothing. Take, for instance, what happened just last month to the CEO of Red Inc., which is the company that just made the new bio-eyes that the military was looking at for the shock troops. Well, just two weeks after Red Inc. got the contract, one of the smaller drug companies came out with a new recreational drug." She continues extracting breakfast, taking coffee rolls out of the bag and setting them on a plate. "At the release party, the Red Inc. CEO was one of the .005% of people 'who may become dependent' and as a result disappeared that night. For six weeks no one knew where he was. They only located him by locking out all of his M.E. cards. They found him stealing other peoples' cards.

Without as much as a gulp of air, she continues, "Well, the military backed out of the deal immediately when the CEO first went missing. Now, to try and save itself, Red Inc. is marketing this product line to law enforcement. That thing was 90% of their projected annual revenue and critical for fueling other product lines." She takes a sip of coffee; the driver mirrors her movement unwittingly. This conversation doesn't seem to be boring the driver, so Remmington continues, "Some of the force are considering it. I know some have had it done, but it is hard to tell, because unlike the old bio-eyes, these look like real eyes. Red Inc. says they work just great, but if you read the fine print, sometimes the lights have gone out—there is a .0002% failure rate—leaving you totally blind."

"Have the lights gone out for anyone on the force?" asks the driver.

"No, not yet. But that would definitely be a career-ending moment. Okay, a couple of business things, and then I want to know more about you. First, at some point today, we have to go get our vehicle. Second, you have to see a medical examiner before next week—can't afford to have any 'defectives' working around here. Finally—now tell me about yourself, because I couldn't get any information from your file."

"You read my file?" The driver wouldn't have been surprised if the answer were yes; after all, *This is a curious one.*

"No, the Cap wouldn't let me, and I couldn't hack my way into reading it," Remmington says with obvious disappointment in her voice. "They've increased a lot of security. I guess I've done that too much, so they had to." She smiles with some sense of pride.

"Well, if you had read my file, it wouldn't have told you much anyways, because there isn't much to tell."

Remmington interrupts, "So, dish! What *is* to tell?" She leans forward toward the driver as if in anticipation of being told the secrets of life.

The driver continues as though they hadn't noticed the outburst, "I have done a couple years here and there."

"Okay, do these '*here and there*' have names? Where did you work last?"

Misleading my new partner is no way to start off our partnership, but if I tell her the truth it could get her killed, which is no way to start off the partnership, either. The driver thinks that this is funny and smiles mildly to themself.

"I was working in Tixe Tower City. The jungle around the city is amazingly beautiful and incredibly dangerous." The driver watches Remmington's eyes grow large with intensity, waiting for the story to unravel.

"Between people falling off the city and the dangers from the jungle, there really wasn't much work there," the driver explains vaguely, twisting the truth. *The people there learn how to be as dangerous as the jungle.*

"You might have moved to the desert, but you haven't left the jungle," Remmington interjects. "I myself have never been to Tixe Tower City, but I did grow up in the wild. Which I hear compares to the jungles of Tixe Tower City. You see, I was an unauthorized birth, so when my parents couldn't make it to the City to have me, I was born and lived the first eight years of my life in the wild." She lowers her tone, as if ashamed of her past. Moving the conversation forward, she asks, "Where did you grow up? Was your family able to get a licensing for you?"

Trying to expedite the bond needed for this partnership, the driver tells a perverted view of the truth, "So, I guess that means we both had a role in the regulations on birthing being so strictly enforced now. Yeah? I wasn't born in the jungle; it was more like the growing plains area. The Council keeps the growing plains pretty primitive." *Unlike your role, my role has nothing to do with where I was born.* The driver turns to get a drink of water, feeling confident that this story will suffice.

"Well if *that's* the case, do you have any siblings?" Remmington beams with the prospect of having commonality with her new partner. She pushes the subject by adding, "My parents tried to get a license for my brother, but by the time it was granted, my mom had lost him to a fever. We left the jungle for good after that and moved here. My parents are still here."

"I'm fairly sure that my parents have passed away at this point. I'm not sure, but I think I have a sister. I was discovered as being unauthorized," the driver then lowers their voice for emphasis, "before the magic age of seven. My parents had to pay the fines for my birth, which left them no choice but for me to be raised by the Order. Now I'm a civil servant, working on paying back the rest of the debt owed." *That one isn't so bad; the only part that isn't true is the age at which I was folded into the Order.*

"How can you not know if you have a sister?" There is intensity in that question, but she is distracted, too. "Wait—can we talk about this on the way in to work? And do you mind if I stop by my desk real quick before we go get the vehicle set up?" queries Remmington as she bites into her bagel.

"Yes, that should work. Did it rain last night, or did I just dream that?"

Moving the food around in her mouth to answer, Remmington replies, "Nope. It's the desert. It doesn't rain often." She begins toward the door and motions for the driver to follow.

"Mickey," a low, whispery voice calls out from the shadows.

Mickey's eyes snap open; even in a whisper, Mickey is well aware of who it is. He is alert but paralyzed with fear. He instantly breaks out in a sweat. The dealer reaches for the firearm under his pillow, not the recommended place to keep it, but it comes in handy at moments like these.

"Mickey," the voice says again, but this time, it is as if the voice is whispering into Mickey's ear. The dealer jerks his massive frame upright and fires two shots toward the foot of the bed—one to each corner of the room. The flares of the weapon illuminate only parts of the room, and with each flash, only half of the dark figure's twisted smile appears, revealing pleasure at seeing Mickey—a man who is a master of his occupation—unhinged and firing wildly into the dark. Mickey pants, stunned to see the dark figure.

Footsteps can be heard coming from down the hall. Mickey starts yelling, "No, stop! Don't come in here!"

"Boss, is everything okay?" the guard calls out as he opens the door. Crossing the threshold, he catches a glimpse of the dark figure looming over the bed. "What the fu—"

In a fluid, lightning-fast motion, the dark figure backhands the gun out of Mickey's hand and fires one round into the sentry's head. The body falls back into the hallway with that twisted smile still pointing at Mickey and the gun pointing at the doorway.

"Stop! Stop! Everybody stop!" Mickey orders.

The rest of the sentries stop outside the door, where the blood is beginning to pool. They stand clear of the open door so as to avoid becoming the next donors to the creeping red.

Mickey tells the remaining guards as calmly as he can, "I'm fine. Now, go back down the hall. I'll call you if I need ya." With no argument, the guards go back to their posts, making almost as much noise as when they were rushing to assist their boss.

"Nice to see y-you again," Mickey stammers.

"I need some equipment."

"Of course. What kind?"

"The typical things." It is clear they've done this dance before. "How fast can you arrange them?"

Trying to gather his wits, Mickey answers, "One, two days tops."

"Which is it: one or two days?" the dark figure responds with irritation in their voice, seizing Mickey's lungs once again.

"Two—two days," Mickey quickly spits out.

"All right, then," the dark figure replies, all irritation instantly vanishing. Within milliseconds, the riled atmosphere seems to have dissipated. "Oh, Mickey?" The dark figure kneels down so that they are at eye level. "I need a vehicle, Mickey.

Can I have one?" It's a mocking pout, but Mickey isn't in the mood to grin.

Mickey looks at the dark figure and then leans over to one side to see the body of his dead guard. The blood is beginning to congeal. He looks to the dark figure and deadpans, "Take Simon's. He ain't gonna use it anymore."

"How many more must litter the floor?" the dark figure rhymes quietly as they move toward Simon's body. Mickey, hearing the playful question, starts to scramble and fumble out of bed, losing sight of the dark figure.

"Let 'em through!" Mickey screams. Mickey looks at the body of his guard. The dark figure has vanished at this point.

"Someone get this shit cleaned up!" he barks. The remaining guards scramble down the hall, surveying for any signs of the deadly intruder. The massive man gets out of bed and heads to his shower. There is more than one pile of shit to clean up.

Mickey steps into the stream of water contemplating how he warranted this relationship. *Shit ... why the hell do they still call me "Mickey"? Not like I've changed it in the twenty years since we met. Not like it's hard to say. José fucking Palmer. It's been that my whole life. Shit ... what a fucking day. A special-order shipment was late, and one of my customers tried to weasel out of a deal. Dumb fuck.*

Mickey soaps up his head. *Well maybe that wasn't so bad. Actually, that was lots of fun, since I got to try out my new toy to make the deal go my way.*

Fu-u-uck. Even in his head, the word seems to have a lot more syllables than it actually does. *I wonder what the body count is gonna be this time. Are they ever gonna call me by my real name?* The arms dealer sighs as he lets the cleansing water wash over his sizable body. *Life wasn't always this messy*, he recalls.

The lift door slides open to the twenty-third floor, and Ben stands directly in front of the doors in anticipation, waiting for Remmington and her new partner. He looks like an anxious puppy craving attention.

"Hey, Ben ...!?" Remmington challenges, raising an eyebrow to indicate her dissatisfaction with his demeanor and location. "Should we get off on a different floor?"

Ben pauses, realizing he is crowding the lift's opening, and he quickly steps aside, granting them access to the floor. "Did you ask yet?" he pants nervously, his eyes twitching back and forth between the two, as though trying to read a document in low light. The driver finally steps off the elevator and joins the other two.

"Yeah, we began talking about it on our way here, but ... we kind of got caught up in introductions, and I knew we were coming into the office, so—" Remmington answers, but Ben cuts her off.

"Oh, that's just fine!" Ben blurts, excitement shining in his bio-mechanical eyes, his voice reaching octaves he hadn't intended. "Don't worry about it; I'll just ask now."

Remmington smiles while patting him on the arm. "Okay, let me go to my desk. I have to grab something real quick."

"Okay, we can walk and talk at the same time," Ben replies, with less fervor.

Ben directs his attention to the driver, as Remmington leads the way with the two of them following behind. "I need to ask a favor of you," he begins. It is obvious he is quite nervous asking favors from complete strangers. There is no point in making him any more self-conscious, so the driver patiently nods. "I've already asked the Captain not to put you on anything two months from today. I've done this because I want to ask you to escort my sister to a gala." Ben takes a gulp of air and seems to be pleased that he got that far without fainting.

With a puzzled look, the driver says, "Go on."

Ben continues, becoming more tense, "It's a—it's a big event, and I intended to ask Remmie, but—but she's on security there, a-and I'm on exhibition, and—and—and—quite frankly, there's no one else available on the force that night." He blurts out, "So, what I'm gonna ask you—"

"He wants you to be his sister's bodyguard, or escort, or whatever he wants to call it," Remmington mercifully interrupts with an audible huff, from under her desk, where she is searching for whatever she is "just grabbing."

"Yes! That's exactly what I'm asking for!" Ben nods enthusiastically.

The driver continues to look puzzled. "Okay, but if the whole force is going to be there, then why does she need extra protection?"

"It's really for our parents' peace of mind," Ben answers, glancing down at Remmington under the desk. His gaze drifts back to the driver, as he continues with the question, "Have you heard of the artist Utionary?" Inhaling deeply, he declares without waiting for a response, "That's my sister." He pauses, trying to assess the driver's acuity on the subject. "I don't know how much you follow the music industry—do you understand how the music regulations work?" Ben calms down enough to finally wait for a reply. It seems important that the driver understand the nuances of the music industry.

"Aren't there two ways to pay an artist?" the driver begins. "Like one credit for or one credit against? I don't know; I don't buy new music." Figuring Ben knows this subject much better, the driver lets their voice trail off in an attempt to emphasize a true lack of knowledge on the subject.

"Kind of," Ben responds. "An artist receives a license from the government that's good for five years. The artist has those five years to make a net value of either a positive million credits or negative million credits. If they make a positive net million, then they can renew their license indefinitely. Those who don't make a positive or negative million cannot renew their license *ever*. But those who have a negative net million must cease being an artist, and they are compensated for it, depending on how poorly they did."

"Mostly 'cause no one will give them a job after they sucked so bad," Remmington cuts in.

"That's probably true," Ben admits, not minding the explanatory assist.

"So, what does this have to do with your sister again?" the driver asks, to refocus the conversation.

"Well, as I said, she's the artist Utionary," Ben says. "She has the record for getting to the negative million credits the quickest. She actually has earned over a *billion* negative credits." He continues proudly, "Which makes her a celebrity," adding soberly, "which also makes our parents nervous when she's invited to big parties like this."

25

"So, what exactly do I have to do?" the driver inquires, trying not to sound put out.

Before Ben can answer, the Cap's voice booms. "Remmington!" There is no mistake in his timbre; Cap is either very angry with her or he has a job for her to do.

Either way, Remmington is startled by the sharpness of his voice, which causes her to hop up and face toward his office. "Yes, sir!" she responds crisply.

The Cap walks over to them. "I need you two to go and investigate a crash," he gruffly hands her a report tablet; she instantly starts to examine it. "There are five people dead and two injured," he continues. "A couple witnesses are still alive, but you need to get there right away." Speaking in general terms to everyone present, he offers thoughtfully, "No one's sure how long they'll last."

"G2!" Remmington swears under her breath.

She closes the open drawers to her desk, hands the report tablet to Ben, and asks, "Will you please call in a transport vehicle and find out what support is there already? I would do it, but we still haven't been to set up our vehicle yet."

"Yeah, I can do that for you," Ben replies, moving back to his work area, dissatisfied with the lack of a definitive solution to his personal dilemma.

The driver and Remmington bypass the locker rooms, since changing into a full uniform would take too long, and the information on the report is grave for the two injured witnesses. Remmington explains this to the driver on the quick trip to the vehicle launch center. This is a massive room with only a couple of vehicles in it. The front ends of all of them are pointing toward the center of the room. All of the vehicles are black, with rounded, wide front ends that dramatically taper to the aft of the vehicle.

Making a starburst, the driver thinks, *but it would have to be a black star.*

Remmington asks, "Which one?" to no one in particular.

Looking at them quickly, without any distinctive difference, the driver starts to walk over to them. The vehicle to the driver's right opens up, startling both of them. Remmington relaxes when she sees a silver leg come out of the opening. The sight of the leg has the opposite effect on the driver, who takes a defensive stance.

A tall man of African and Asiatic heritage emerges from the vehicle. He is in his late twenties, and both his left leg and right arm are a brilliant metallic silver. The uniform he wears is all black, making the man's head seem out of place, with his soft almond eyes and round cheeks. The end of his nose is twisted down and to the left. He has a small square patch of hair on his chin, but the rest of his head is completely hairless, with not even eyebrows. This unnerves the driver a little.

As this visually stunning man steps out of his vehicle, he greets Remmington with a wave and calls out, "Yo, Rem. Yours is that one," pointing to a vehicle that is two to his right.

"Thank you, Cass. I could never tell them apart." She smiles and waves. She gives the driver a nudge toward the vehicle indicated.

As they near the vehicle it opens up, giving the driver the ability to see inside. Looking inside, the driver can see that the seats are laid all the way back. The two partners climb in on opposite sides. As they lie down in them, the seats start to adjust to their bodies. The vehicle calls out as adjustments are completed.

"Back angle—Completed.

"Seat angle—Completed.

"Seat height—Completed.

"Lumbar support—Completed.

"Lateral neck support—Completed."

"This will only take a minute, but then we won't have to do this again," Remmington volunteers. "As long as you don't wreck the vehicle," she adds with a smile.

"How did you know that was my evil plan?" the driver jokes back at her.

To pass the time, the driver ventures an inquiry, "So, is Cass a driver as well?"

Remmington rolls her head to make eye contact. She screws up her whole face before answering, calculating whether she should give the long or short version. "His name is Cassius Dorian, and he is the only one who is a solo driver at this point in time. We were partners when I first started and I was a driver, but that was before his accident." She takes a deep breath and goes back to staring straight ahead. "I had a medical issue that laid me up for a little while, and the powers that be set him up with a new partner. They then grounded me after I came back to work. He and his new partner stayed together." She stops talking, turning her head toward her window, and looks to be deep in thought.

"How did he end up like that?" the driver asks gently. "You don't have to tell me."

"No, it's okay; he doesn't mind other people knowing what happened," she replies, turning to the computer's keyboard. "It's better to explain with visuals." She enters the pertinent data as the adjustments drone on:

"Pressure points—Completed.

"Leg length—Completed.

"Foot width—Completed.

"Ankle rotation limiter—Completed."

Light flashes over the front window, and a light green side view of two vehicles appears; there is a distance meter between them. Remmington begins the narration in her official tone, "Cassius and his partner were responding to a corporate theft. The perpetrators' vehicle didn't respond to the disruptor shots." As she says this, two balls of blue light leave the front of the pursuing vehicle and hit the lead vehicle. "This is thought to be what provoked the perpetrators, or they could have just then discovered how to work the property they had stolen. It is unclear. They fired one Spydertech Plura or 'spider' missile at Cassius." A short red line leaves the lead vehicle and moves toward the trailing vehicle. As it crosses the distance, it splits into eight smaller red lines that spread out and then angle toward Cassius's vehicle.

Remmington continues the narrative, "Cassius tried to maneuver the vehicle out of the way of the missiles and could only slide his side of the vehicle toward the missiles in an attempt to protect his partner when it was clear his evasive maneuver had failed." Her voice loses a bit of its authoritarian bravado, "Unfortunately, with the angle that the missiles hit, they all struck the far side of the vehicle, killing Cassius's partner and riddling Cassius's body with shrapnel and leaving him with burns covering 64% of his body. The review of this event has shown that there was a 98% chance of this outcome being unavoidable and only a 0.5% chance of completely avoiding any of the missiles. An overwhelming majority of the outcomes showed that both of them should have been killed."

As she finishes the report, the adjustments to their seats also complete, and the vehicle comes alive.

The driver asks, "Were the perpetrators apprehended?"

"To this day they're still at large, and the stockpile of spider missiles is unaccounted for. Some think they could have been shipped off-planet or to the Green Glass region. But none have been used here again. Also, the company that makes spider missiles won't give us an accounting letting us know how many were stolen," Remmington has lost her official tone and now sounds more irritated than anything, "Or even the basic information about this weapon system, because they're protected by the corporate laws. We do know that they haven't sold many of this type of missile system," Remmington finishes.

As soon as the driver takes the controls, the vehicle launches.

Thick dust clouds fill the air as their vehicle approaches the crash site. The café where the crash took place is on the twenty-eighth floor of the Nolispe Tri Towers Number 1. The driver sets the vehicle on the twenty-seventh-floor outdoor parking area.

As they walk up the outdoor pathway, a building security guard stops them, announcing, "Sorry, no one can go this way. Please find an alternate route around the café." The young man is clean-shaven.

"We are here to investigate the crash," the driver responds as Remmington flashes her ID.

"I see. Well, be careful—there's debris all the way up the walkway," the guard says as he steps aside.

"Thank you. Has anyone else tried to go this way?" Remmington asks as she passes.

"No, I think most people are up in the hallway. They're watching through the interior doors to the café," the guard responds with confidence.

Walking up doesn't take very long using the outdoor switchback ramps, but the guard was accurate with his warning about the debris. Parts of chairs and tables litter the walkway, with chunks of the building mixed in, as well. The amount and size of building rubble increases exponentially as they reach the twenty-eighth floor.

They both stop at the top of the ramp to make an assessment of the crash site before moving onto the outdoor patio. The café's seating is divided. A curved, forty-foot-long glass wall was twenty feet tall in the middle and tapered down to twelve feet on the sides. Large sections of the glass wall contribute to the carnage. Their discerning eyes identify two types of tables in the wreckage and a few surviving tables near the perimeter. There are small round tables for two people and square tables that could comfortably seat up to four people at a time. Some of the square outdoor tables have spiral covers that operate in the same fashion as Japanese folding fans for blocking out the sun or light rain. On this day, the spirals are reversed and the cover folded on itself into a two-inch-wide arm. From where the driver and Remmington stand, the interior door is to their right as they view it through the glass wall, and it makes up one third of the back wall of the café. The other two thirds is counter space and display areas for the café.

It is a mess, but unlike a bomb explosion, where there is a center to the destruction and usually nothing remains in that area, there is destruction in many different directions; only a few apparently random things are untouched by the catastrophe. A luxury vehicle rests upright, partly sticking out of the inside of the café's indoor seating area.

In the middle of the chaos, a lone woman stands with her back to them. She is fixated on her task of setting up some kind of equipment, unaware that they have arrived on scene. She is tall and thin, with a small build. She has long light-brown hair in a single tight braid. Her gray-tan jumpsuit accentuates the auburn strands in her hair.

Even from behind, Remmington recognizes her and calls out, "Can we come onto the scene yet, Aly?"

Aly quickly spins around to face them, whipping her braid so that it lands over her shoulder on her front left side. She smiles and calls back, "Hey, Remmie! I just finished setting up for the scan. Come on over, and I can try to make sense of all this. Is this your new partner? Did the Cap give you the 'new blood' speech?"

"I don't think the speech covered this sort of thing for my first day," the driver answers, as they walk over to Aly, trying not to disturb too much. The dust still in the air causes Aly to have a little sneezing fit just as the driver and Remmington come closer.

"Are you okay?" Remmington asks as the driver sneezes as well.

"Not you, too!" Aly jokes. "One second, and we can start the scans of the site and search of the vehicle."

From this vantage point, they can see the entire café and all of the entrances and exits, as well. There is an employee doorway to a back work area, the pathway up to the patio that the driver and Remmington came from, and a path that descends from the higher floors. The main internal entrance is mostly a glass wall with large glass doors. Two guards are standing at the closed door, controlling who comes in or goes out. A sizable crowd of onlookers has assembled outside the café; there is a face gawking at the destruction from almost every open space of window.

Destruction is like flames to a moth, the driver ponders inwardly, scanning the crowd, wondering if the creator of this mess is standing out in the horde of moths admiring his or her work.

Just then, the driver recognizes an odd, dark hairstyle. Next to the unusual hair, and bobbing up and down in the crowd, is a head of moppy blond hair. The driver had seen these two geniuses before; they are Rick and Jeff, the station attendants from the isolation zone. The driver turns to point them out to Remmington, and in the second that the driver's eyes are off the two, they have melted into the crowd and sea of faces.

The egg-shaped pieces of equipment Aly had set up hover and cross over each other's paths, dancing over all the destruction. Aly studies the tablet she is holding, making adjustments to the paths that some of the scanners are traveling in order to expedite the scan. When Aly finishes, she looks up and smiles at both of them, as most of the scanners return to their carrying post, which is a meter and a half tall and has holes in it that perfectly accommodate the scanners. The post will assume the look of an ordinary cylinder if all the scanners have returned.

Aly leads the way over to the vehicle, with four scanners in tow. "The back passenger, here, is the only door that can be opened, because the rest have been damaged too much," she informs them as she opens that door to let the scanners in. Almost as quickly as they enter the vehicle, all the scanners leave. Two glide to the carrying post, while the other two hover around, scanning and waiting for more instructions.

Aly reviews the scans on her tablet, and Remmington reads over her shoulder, as the driver enters the vehicle to see with their own eyes. The scans tell Aly and Remmington the same thing that the driver discovers. There was no one in the vehicle when the crash occurred, evident by the complete lack of any blood or interior damage caused by a body to the vehicle. Additionally, there is an unusual hole in the center dash that is not connected to damage caused by the crash. The driver crawls into the front to get a better look at this hole.

Remmington asks, "What would've caused that?" as she points to the tablet's report that highlighted the dash damage.

Aly replies, "I'm not sure, but I think it's pre-crash."

"I think it caused the crash to be possible," the driver calls out. With this, both Remmington and Aly stick their heads into the back seat to see what the driver is up to. The driver has an arm in the hole up to at least the elbow. "There is nothing there," the driver says, confirming the obvious with a puzzled tone.

"That is about where the ACC is on this type of vehicle," Remmington says.

Aly gives her a puzzled look.

The driver clarifies for Aly's benefit, "Anticrash computer. It's an independent system to give the vehicle another level of protection from failure."

"So, someone removed it?" Aly asks.

"It must have been done while driving. They broke the dash to get at it," Remmington theorizes as she points to the surrounding damage on the dash.

The driver and Aly nod their heads in agreement.

"Would you hit the release of the front and back hatches, so I can finish the scans?" Aly asks as she removes her head from the vehicle.

The driver searches and quickly finds both releases and then goes back to examining the hole in the dash.

Aly calls out, "All the scans are done. Ready for playback." She signals that Remmington and the driver should come join her.

They both exit the vehicle and wait with Aly for the playback to start. All of the scanners leave the carrying post and move to different areas. To the driver and Remmington, there is no discernible pattern.

"Okay, ready?" Aly asks.

Without waiting for a response, the scanners start to project what the scene looked like before the crash. Everything, from the walls and tables to the people, is displayed to look as if nothing had happened there. The projection even makes the vehicle less noticeable, although it remains less than fifteen feet away from them.

The scene starts to play out the recreated events, showing people moving, and off in the distance the vehicle can be seen coming into the outdoor patio area. It bounces off the patio twice before crashing into the glass windows and into two women talking at the table closest to the windows, killing them instantly. The vehicle continues and crashes into part of the back counter, hitting a café worker and bouncing off the back wall. Sliding along a different path back toward the windows, the ricocheting vehicle clips another customer, killing him, after which it finally stops in its current position.

"The replay was at one-third real time," Aly informs them as she makes adjustments on her tablet.

"Where did the fifth person die?" asks the driver. "I didn't see it."

"Let me see," Aly muses, dragging out the words as if asking a question as well. She looks over the tablet again, restarting the replay from the part where the vehicle crashes into the window and stopping it before the vehicle crashes into the counter.

"There!" she exclaims with satisfaction, pointing and following the action with her finger. "It hits and shatters a couple of chairs. That sends parts of the chairs into this group of people along the side of the café, where the larger parts impale this worker, here," Aly explains as she highlights the worker and his injuries.

"Where are the two that survived?" Remmington asks Aly.

Looking over her tablet, Aly responds, "They are both at the same medical center, in critical condition and nonresponsive." She confirms, "At the Lazarus Center, downtown."

"We may not have the operator of the vehicle, but we *do* have the registration for the vehicle," Aly adds as both the driver and Remmington move to leave. "One Simon O. Larsen is listed on the registration, but that is all I can tell you from here. You will have to wait for me to get back, before I can file a full report with the scans; they should tell us who was really driving at the time of the crash."

"Thanks. Are you done with everything we will need, so we can let the cleanup group in?" Remmington asks.

"Just packing up now. Here, give this to Ben to load, and that should get you the full report sooner," Aly suggests as she hands her tablet over to the driver.

The twenty-third floor of the Civil Central Command is bustling with people moving between the only four doors on the floor as the lift opens—contrary to when the driver first arrived. Ben is behind the counter when they walk into the waiting area. His manner is nothing like it was only a few hours ago, when he asked the driver for help. Now Ben looks to be down to business, with a strange intensity about the task at hand. The task at hand commences when Remmington hands him Aly's tablet without a word. Remmington leads the driver back to Cap's office, where they find the Cap sitting on the couch reading a book. He places it on the table as they walk in. The driver reads the title on the spine of the book: *Seeds.* The cover is a blank hardbound surface with a stylized emblem unfamiliar to the driver. *Strange topic for the Cap.* The driver amuses themself with visions of the Cap out in the garden with a sunbonnet on, knowing full well the subject of the book is other than it seems.

"How bad was it?" asks the Cap as he gestures for them to have a seat.

Remmington answers, "Ben is loading the data into the

system now." She sits down in a chair to the left of the driver. "So, hopefully we will get more information on Simon O. Larsen." She finishes the thought, "The name on the vehicle's registration."

Cap interjects, "But who was operating the vehicle?"

"We could find no one," the driver offers. "The on-scene data scans and physical evidence leave us with a blank as to who the operator was."

Remmington continues, "With what we saw, Aly's equipment indicates there was no operator of the vehicle at the time of the crash. We theorize," looking to the driver for affirmative support and then back to the Cap, "that the crash was possible because the ACC was removed sometime before the crash, while the vehicle was in motion."

Remmington looks intently at the Cap, waiting for his perspective on the situation. The Cap, having been sitting with his arms folded, listening to Remmington, now unfolds his arms and twists the dark gray band on his left ring finger as he looks up in thought, trying to see in his mind's eye how that would be possible. After a few moments, he leans forward, slaps the tops of his knees and pushes himself up to a standing position. "Well! Let's go see what Ben has discovered," he says matter-of-factly. "Maybe he can tell us how long it'll be until he's done," the Cap suggests as he moves to the door with Remmington and the driver in tow.

The three of them find Ben in an evidence-processing lab. Each processing lab is a rectangle with three workstations. The station at the end of the room is off-center to the right, with a door on the left and a glass wall behind the station for viewing the adjacent multipurpose room, where physical evidence is examined and scanned and interrogations are conducted. Ben is sitting in the center of the bank of screens at the end of the room, with his back to the door. Data is streaming across the screens as he rapidly scans back and forth, trying to understand what is passing by him. The speed at which the information is passing is far beyond a normal human's visual capacity, but this does not deter Ben from trying.

Without turning around at the sound of his visitors, he waves a hand in acknowledgement. As they approach Ben's position, all the screens blink off and then flash back on again. This is rapidly followed by a weak flicker and everything shutting off, including the lights in the hallway. After being unexpectedly cast into darkness, the three of them remain still; it is almost painfully dark for them. As they stand frozen, they can hear Ben moving around on the other side of the room.

"Does this happen often here in the City?" the driver inquires.

"Oh, you're funny," Remmington says. Then, "Ben? ... Ben? Where are you?"

There is a rustling sound and the sound of a small metal door opening. "Well, I'm checking the electrical panel for the room," Ben calls out in as comforting a tone as he can muster. With a bit of confusion evident in his tone, he continues, "From what I can tell, there seems to be nothing wrong here." Ben can now be heard opening the drawers of the desk, clearly looking for something. "Hold on! I'll get some lights," he says in a quieter voice so as not to startle them as he passes by on his way to the door. Because the power is out, the doors will not open automatically. Ben has to manually crank them open with a handle he retrieves from the drawer. It is obvious that he's done this before. Ben concludes the procedure and continues down the hall.

The three colleagues Ben has left in the dark stand perfectly still so as not to fall into anything. Conversation is curtailed as they hear a *thunk* and a soft "G2" from someone in the hall stubbing a toe in the pitch-black environment, searching for an exit from the building. The lab is situated in the center of the building, so there are no exterior windows to allow in natural light, making navigation virtually impossible.

Ben, however, moves like a cat through this ebony soup, and in less than a minute, he returns with two old-style Surefire flashlights and one standard issue Nova Beam lantern. Ben's face is illuminated by the Nova Beam as he reenters the lab. Obviously, he is pleased with himself as he offers the Cap his choice of the three lights. He then turns to Remmington and the driver, handing them each one of the remaining light sources.

"See? Two months' salary is finally paying off," Ben says to Remmington with a proud gesture toward the Surefire flashlights.

"Ben, can you show me what you were looking at over here?" Cap calls over from the electrical panel, completely oblivious to the conversation going on behind him.

The driver leans toward Remmington and whispers, "Two months of salary for what? Both flashlights?" The issue seems to lack merit, considering the current situation.

"No! Each one was two months' salary, and I've been giving him shit for buying the second one," Remmington shares in a whisper to answer the driver's questions. She giggles; it seems appropriate to her to torment Ben whenever possible when it comes to his eccentric purchases.

"Well, not much we can gain here. Let's go find out where there is power and see how much is affected," the Cap suggests after a couple more moments looking over the panel in the dark.

They move back to the main area of the twenty-third floor by the lift to find most of the personnel who work on the floor standing around in the dark, with the lifts inoperable. Over the next ten minutes, as more people get lanterns and communicate with people on other floors, it becomes clear that power has been knocked out in the entire Civil Central Command, starting with the twenty-third floor. Crews scurry up and down the stairwells, trying to determine the cause of the outage. There seems to be safety in numbers and with all this activity about, surely a solution will be found. But none of the connections are damaged. None of the backup power systems are performing correctly, and everything looks as if it should be working, yet no one can determine the reason why there is no power of any kind in the Civil Central Command.

As quickly as the power went out, and for still-unknown reasons, the power comes back on forty-two minutes later, as if by design. The crowd disperses as a search is initiated to find out how any of this is possible and whether it might happen again. Ben is placed in charge of the team that will investigate the twentieth through the twenty-eighth floors.

Aly is delayed by the blackout when she returns from the scene, and she is heading to take over Ben's analysis of the scans. She arrives on the twenty-third floor just as Ben is leaving to start his investigation. Aly covertly guides Ben by his left arm off to the side before he can leave, smiling at him as she does so.

"Wha—? Are you all right?" Ben asks in a whisper, somewhat bewildered, as he realizes who has just moved him.

Still smiling, Aly says, "Yeah. I'm not afraid of the dark." She continues, in hushed tones, "Do you know what happened yet?"

"No!" Ben replies. "We're just getting underway with our investigation. I was on my way out to investigate all of the junction points on the twentieth to the twenty-eighth floors."

"So—how did your sight work out?" Aly presses with some excitement.

"I was the only one who could see for the first couple of minutes," Ben confides. "It was really cool, because everything just looked a little darker in shade. I mean, it was like when I tested them when I got them, but way cooler, since I didn't expect it," Ben answers with a happy, nervous smile.

"*G-squared!* That's just how they said they would work," says Aly, her enthusiasm radiating from her. She holds both of his forearms and squeezes. They continue moving past each other, rotating around, almost as if in a dance.

Remmington is standing on the other side of the room, smiling at Aly. Aly makes her way over to her and asks, "What is that smile about?"

"Smile? Me? What are you talking about?" Remmington playfully mocks.

Aly frowns, "Remmie, you know better. I was just asking how far he got before the power went out. That's all."

"Yes, and the swearing was because of how little he got done, right?" Remmington quizzes; her laugh removes any seriousness in her accusation.

"That was *not* mad swearing, and you know it! And we will just have to see how much was done—you know how Ben can be sometimes. He is a little anxious sometimes," Aly says in hopes of ending the conversation there as she moves past Remmington.

Letting Aly pass and lead the way, Remington points out in a long, drawn-out breath, "You know, Ben was anything but anxious since we returned with your tablet." She lets that hang in the air for a while before she follows up with, "In fact, I would say he focuses more when things involve you."

This is not where Aly wants this conversation to go right now, and she hopes being a few steps ahead of Remmington is enough to hinder Remmington's view of the red flush growing across her face. The two of them walk in this manner all the way to the evidence-processing lab, where the Cap and the driver are waiting, still discussing the possible causes of the outage.

Turning at the sound of their entrance, the Cap is surprised to see Aly's condition and inquires, "Aly, did you run here? You are all red in the face." He seems truly concerned.

Remmington smiles and answers, "I caught her just as she got here. She sure looked like she was in a rush for something." Aly glares back at Remmington, not knowing if she is being sarcastic or helpful, but Remmington's quiet smile tells her where they stand, and Aly recovers with a warm smile.

"I appreciate your hustle and enthusiasm," the Cap says with a light pat on Aly's back. "Let's get back to it, then," he concludes as he gestures toward the now-powered-up bank of screens.

Aly takes the seat Ben had occupied, as the other three grab chairs in the room and gather around her. While the three of them sit quietly, Aly starts to mutter to herself.

The driver asks, "Is everything all right?"

"No. I don't get it," Aly answers and starts to mutter to herself once again.

Remmington jokes, "What did Ben mess—"

She is cut off by the Cap's interruption, "Aly, what don't you understand?" His intonation makes it clear he is putting an end to all joking.

"Well, sir, I have started a search for the files that Ben had loaded from the tablet. There are none. So I started searching the tablet to see if he had uploaded the data yet." Her frustration grows, and she sits back a little in her chair. "The tablet is blank. The tablet has been reset back to the factory setting," Aly reports in a definitive yet bewildered, tone. She sits back all the way, almost slumping.

"Have you been able to check the scanners' memory to see if they have any data?" Remmington asks, hoping to jar her friend's mind into action. She moves to the station on the right side of the room, selecting the seat closest to Aly's station and starting a search of her own. The bank of monitors pops to life.

"I have that search running right now, and I'm waiting for it to finish up," Aly responds, regaining some composure. "But there is something else going on that I don't understand," she confides as she leans into the screen with intensity.

The Cap stands up and positions himself between Aly and Remmington, so he can observe both work stations at the same time. Looking back and forth between them, he asks Remmington to place a report on hold and then asks Aly to do the same thing for a couple of different items on her screens.

Ben shows up in the middle of this, as part of his investigation. Aly and Remmington spin out of their seats and start toward

Ben. Cap halts their forward progress by calling Ben over to Aly's bank of screens and ordering him to sit down.

"Cap, I'm not done with my investigation," Ben explains, holding the back of the seat that he was ordered into, not quite ready to succumb to his leader's wishes. "I still have two floors to hear the report on," Ben weakly protests. Without looking away from the screens, the Cap points to the seat with an open hand.

Ben takes the seat, and Cap asks, "Show me where you loaded the tablet, please." With a bewildered look, Ben searches for the files he loaded earlier.

"Where did they go?" Ben asks. "I have found some empty shells that should have the raw data in them, but there is nothing—not even a time stamp for when I created them." His confusion is mixed with real frustration.

"That's what we've been trying to figure out," the Cap retorts as he looks at Remington's screens.

"Cap, what are you seeing?" the driver asks, noticing the Cap is zeroing in on something.

The Cap moves to Ben's screens and starts to explain, "Well, here ..." He then returns to Remmington's screens and points out some of his findings, "Here! This report was logged in this morning at the start of Ben's shift and is just fine." The Cap points to a different screen. "This is when you and Remmie logged into and adjusted your vehicle. Here ..." walking over to the other bank of screens, "this is the last report that they have found that is correct—it's the report tablet I handed Remmie about the crash. Yet everything else is corrupted or not there." The captain steps back from the group, as if to make an announcement. With his arms outstretched, he exclaims, "I personally know that there are at least thirty reports from this department that should have been generated for this type of incident."

Ben starts typing and asks, "What about the reports from the other departments?"

Aly is quicker, "There is nothing. In fact, there are no reports or logs of any kind for what looks like thirty minutes before the blackout. If anything was entered during that time, it is apparently lost."

Warehouse Sixteen has been empty for the better portion of three decades. In the history of this derelict building, there have been various dealings—some good, some bad. For a short time it was used as a nightclub, and now José is toying with the idea of reopening it as one called Silver Bullet. But today is not the day to daydream about such things, for if today doesn't go well, that idea would be moot.

José signals a guard to join him. Matt Levingston is the man José has put in charge of the security for this deal. Immediately Matt rushes to his boss's side.

"You made sure this place was completely locked down? We can't have anyone other than them—I mean, our guest— getting in, right?" José asks, wiping the sweat from his brow. The waiting is more nerve-racking then anything else. The guard nods affirmatively and takes up a parade rest while waiting for business to be conducted.

Matt Levingston is competent in the eyes of José. Part of this is related to Matt being seven years José's senior. Matt is just short of being average height and is beginning to show the spread of middle age. His thin, light-brown hair is thinning and is brushed straight back; there is no hint of gray. Matt's mustache is always kept impeccably groomed at a medium length. Somehow, this helps maintain his tough-guy look when he is mad about something and the hair on his head gets messed up. It's the kind of look wanted for security personnel. But his real asset to José is his experience and discretion pertaining to the Green Glass Zone.

José is not normally a nervous fellow, but with today's pressure, he is sweating more than usual. *Hopefully this is gonna end on a good note,* José thinks as he pats Matt on the shoulder and starts to pace again.

"Sir, I have my best men on this operation. Nothing to worry about," Matt replies to José's nervous behavior.

José lets out a brief sigh and moves to pace around a couple of tables. He tries to screw up his courage. *Okay, keep it cool. Everything will be fine. They haven't killed you before, so why now?* José lets out a small chuckle.

While pacing and waiting for the dark figure, the boss spins around on his heels; he has his hand to his face, brushing his knuckles against his lower lip. The other hand reaches across his girth to support his elbow. Deep in contemplation, he fails to notice Matt moving to the other side of the room and resuming his parade-rest stance, with his hands behind his back.

Mind whirling with ghosts of the past, José remembers when he was only a grunt. *If only I had stayed in my house and skipped that meeting twenty years ago,* he muses.

José grew up in one of the tougher areas of the City. In order to survive, he got involved in illegal weapons deals by being a runner for Rachenov, an extraordinarily insidious character who was the most ruthless individual José had ever seen. No one with even half a working brain cell would dare to cross Rachenov. Everyone, from City officials to street toughs, would speak of him in hushed tones, fearful of talking with one of Rachenov's minions or being overheard by one. However, that was before *that day*.

That day started off with José being summoned by Rachenov to meet at the warehouse, where he would routinely get more information about his next errand.

Being the top dealer meant that you were always finely dressed, and Rachenov was that. However, the clothes did not correspond with the man's personality. His whole body was skeletal. Dried by the desert winds, his pale skin was that of a lizard, interrupted with patches of mottled gray and brown. His eyes, the whites of which were a crusty brown, could keep track of all the movements in the room. His hair was rapidly getting thinner. The teeth of the man were a darkish yellow and seemed to have been unnaturally filed to points. His appearance was definitely unnerving, but when it came to business, Rachenov was barbaric. He was no better with basic manners, either. Truly, Rachenov was one of the world's most gruesome characters.

On this particular day, Rachenov was, by all accounts, in a "good mood" when José entered the warehouse and addressed his boss, "What is the package, sir?"

"We'll get to that," Rachenov said, licking his chapped lips and motioning José closer. "What I want to know is, where's the rest of my money from the last deal?"

José felt faint. He knew this could turn into his execution. He could feel his skin begin to burn while the boss stared at him. Rachenov made no sound and was poised as if ready to pounce.

"I turned in all that was given to me for that delivery, sir," José replied, gulping. It was a dry gulp that could be heard clear across the warehouse. Guards turned to watch the encounter; they were pleased it wasn't them.

Rachenov scowled. "No you didn't, you little snot!" He stuck his finger far up his nostril and dug out ... something and flicked it at José. "There's five hundred missing!" He was interrupted by his abettor.

"Sir, your next appointment's here," he said.

"Okay, good," Rachenov replied. He faced José. "Don't move!" he glared and turned away. José appreciated the reprieve and was scrambling to figure out how not to get himself killed, when he was distracted by the dark figure walking into view.

The "next appointment" wore regal clothes. They exuded power and prestige. This person obviously deserved the attention of the top man. José wondered who this person was. Whoever they were, they were important enough to stop one of Rachenov's rants and give José a stay of execution.

The dark figure's black hair was shoulder length and tied back to keep it in order. Those eyes could pierce your very soul and leave you shattered when they released your gaze. These were eyes that Death could use to obliterate one's life.

"So, my friend, what business can I help you with today?" Rachenov asked in his raspy tone.

The dark figure remained silent.

"What?" Rachenov chided. "Need another shipment filled?" the dealer asked in mocking tones. José knew that tone and knew damn well that Rachenov would not satisfy any order placed.

The dark figure then looked at Rachenov with a blazing glare. With lightning speed and machine precision, the dark figure launched a knife that appeared out of nowhere. The dart pierced Rachenov's throat, causing blood to spurt all over the ground. Rachenov's wild eyes widened beyond their capabilities as he grappled with the reality of his miscalculation and struggled for a few seconds, unable to breathe. Rachenov collapsed, twitching involuntarily, and was no more.

The other advisors were taken aback, horrified that their boss, a pillar in the underworld, had been callously murdered before their very eyes. What really threw Rachenov's men off-course was the fact that they were left to deal with this nightmare. This Green Glass religious radical, who had no name, had murdered their crime boss in a room with thirteen others surrounding them. And the fact that the dark figure had done it so quickly, without hesitation, was even more unnerving.

Clearly, this was a person with a death wish, and the advisors were more than willing to fulfill that order for the dark figure. They finally shifted into action and began to draw weapons from underneath their coats.

The dark figure smiled.

Another knife flashed into existence, a weapon of medium length, about eighteen to twenty inches long, with a slight curve. There was a killing edge on both sides, giving it the maximum effectiveness for forward and reverse thrusts. The metal of the blade was a dark black, yet it had a sheen of silver as it glinted in the warehouse light.

The dark figure danced around the room, slicing through throats, chests, arms, anything their knife desired. José stood, paralyzed, in the midst of the chaos unfolding before him. Blood glistened like rubies travelling through the air before splattering against the walls. Screams of hardened men echoed in his ears as he stood watching his taskmasters topple. Shots were fired and lit the room. The copper smell of blood was thick in the air. José felt the blood decorate his face, as well. And all he could do was stare straight ahead.

After an eternal three minutes, the screams stopped, the bullets stopped, the sound of the knife cutting through flesh stopped—everything except for the pounding of his own heart. It was no longer a beat; it was a roar. The pressure in José's chest was so high that his vision had collapsed to a small tunnel. He scanned the room, assessing the bodies of his former slave drivers around his feet. His vision settled on the dark figure standing hunched in the middle of their handiwork, hair completely tousled. Those immaculate clothes of earlier were slightly shifted and twisted but bore surprisingly little blood. In fact, José had more gore on his face than the dark figure did on their whole body. The dark figure licked the few drops of ichor from their lips.

"Looks like you've been promoted, Mickey," the dark figure's lips said wickedly.

"W-what?" José stammered, in shock that he was still standing, knees locked to the point of pain. Silently, the dark figure moved, looking José up and down. All this time, the dark figure was toying with the knife. After about a minute of this examination, the stranger tilted their head to the left and gave a wide, predatory grin. José was even more unnerved.

"I like you," the dark figure said in a soft whisper up against the back of José's neck, putting the knife in their back left pocket. "Oh yes, I think you'll do just fine." The young runner shuddered as the dark figure placed a hand on his shoulder. "Oh yes," the stranger repeated. The dark figure turned away as if speaking to all the dead that were present, "You and I are going to be good friends, Mickey."

There it is again, José thought. He blinked. "What did you call me?"

The dark figure grinned again, ignored José's question, and continued. "You're going to complete the deal that this nihilist—" they said, kicking Rachenov's corpse, "refused to finish. Understood?"

José nodded his head. The stranger grinned wide once more. "Good," they said. The dark figure turned to leave. "Be seeing you, Mickey," the dark figure said and disappeared.

"Mickey." For a brief second, José's recollections seem to have become an auditory hallucination. But the cold voice that the dealer knows all too well is very real and snaps José back to the present as it calls out, "Mickey." The name wafts out across the warehouse, sending a cold chill down José's spine; he spins and sees the dark figure standing before him. In their hand is the leg of a corpse they are dragging behind them with the same nonchalance one might walk a pet.

"G2. You scared me shitless!" the arms dealer exclaims. The dark figure gives José what is, for them, a warm smile.

"Funny. I thought you looked like you would shit at the sight of a mouse right about now," the dark figure replies.

José looks at the dead body. "What the fuck! Your best men?" José yells to the lead security guard, pointing toward the body. Matt dashes across the warehouse and slides up next to José to see the corpse.

"Ah, fuckin' A, man!" he groans. "Sorry, boss, that was the only new recruit here," he explains. "She wasn't even with us for a month yet." Matt throws this in as an afterthought. José and the dark figure give him a confused look.

"She was startled by my arrival and tried to strike me with her firearm ... as if it were possible. That is none of my concern. She was a nihilist," the dark figure announces. "Now, I believe you have some things for me to look at."

"Yes. Right over here; please come this way!" the nervous dealer stammers. "Oh, you can leave that thing there. He will get it," José gestures to the corpse and to the lead security guard.

The dark figure drops the leg of their "new friend," and Matt lays the dead guard on an empty table.

Near the vehicles that had ferried the equipment to the deal are several tables covered in pure white drop cloths that conceal the merchandise. As José approaches, one of his men pulls off a couple of the drop cloths, revealing various small arm weapons.

The dealer gestures to the panoply of items and picks up one small device. "This is a Transtech Needle Slicer," he explains, his spirits now picking up as he talks about things he knows best. After all, this is José's true profession. "You throw it toward an opponent, and when the timer reaches zero, needles sprout and pin the fucker."

The dark figure remains silent, although intrigue shows in their eyes.

José scans the table looking for something he thinks might trigger a response from his audience. He moves on and pulls up one of the pistols, "Now, this bad boy is a Walther Assassin .22-cal. The pistol has a decompression mechanism that suppresses the sound. However, it travels at high velocity, so it can traverse through an object and then still pierce the target in near pristine shape. Real good for offin' someone at the theatre, or anywhere in a crowd, at close range."

"This is good," the dark figure says, examining it. "It feels ...

very good." The contour of the grip fits in their hand perfectly. "What else?" Not trying to sound put off, the dark figure acknowledges that there is a lot more to see.

"Aha, I wanted to show you this badass!" José says gleefully. The resonance in his voice announces his fondness for this next piece of hardware, as he rips off another drop cloth and picks up a gun that is rather large even when compared to his substantial bulk. "This is the improved S.Hi.T. rifle, with all of the bells and whistles. Single shot, four shot, and full auto, with belt-feed conversion. This one has a casing collector—reduces your footprint—adjustable bipod stands, and the latest distance meter/night and day scope made by Red Inc." José strokes the scope with affection. "It can data link to interface with a computer, giving you the ability to do such things as face recognition mapping, or you may want to robotically control this sucker—the possibilities are endless."

José takes another break to calibrate his approach and tries to gauge his impact. While removing the dead security guard, his men bang the doors of the warehouse and distract the dark figure. José feels as if he is losing momentum, and he snaps back into his pitch with what he considers the most impressive feature of this weapon system. "The fact is," he declares loudly, trying to regain the dark figure's attention, "that this weapon system has had other companies trying to copy it. But the real beauty of this thing is the thirty-one different types of specialty rounds that can be used." José finishes with a big smile, gesturing to a stack of ammo boxes sitting on the floor next to the table. "And we've got 'em all!

"Here, let me show you some of what this baby can do," José says as he picks up a clip and moves to a shooting area that his men have set up earlier. "I loaded this clip with a couple of different types of rounds and we have—" José is struck by a brilliant idea as he loads up the weapon. "Hey!" he shouts out to his men fumbling around with the corpse, "Put up that body, over here. It'll show how these rounds work better than the plastic barrel will."

José's men prop the body of the dead girl on the top of target barrel, as José sets the weapon on a far table and loads the clip.

"First round is a normal jacketed round. I am going to aim for the left arm, just below the shoulder," José says as he lines up the shot. The distance is clearly too close for the size of the weapon; at most it is only sixty-five yards, while the gun has an accuracy distance of three miles. As he shoots, a *whoosh* sound and a compression of air that presses against everyone in the vicinity are all the physical signs to evidence that José has fired the weapon. Almost simultaneously, the right arm of the body blows apart just below the shoulder, and the forearm and hand fall to the ground. Laughter breaks out, as the arm makes a squishy slap on the floor.

"I don't think that Red Inc. has made the best scope—or are you really that bad of a shot?" the dark figure jokes, nudging José in the side. His men stand around, keeping their comments to themselves, but they snicker their agreement.

José steps back from the weapon, feeling a bit sheepish. "The scope and rifle work just fine," he declares. He is not in the mood for this embarrassment, "and you know I shoot just fine. I was just talking about *my* left," he states emphatically.

"Sure, sure. Now let me see what the other types of rounds can do," the dark figure says as they move in to take control of the weapon. With a quick lineup and adjustment of the scope, the dark figure fires two single shots downrange, striking the corpse in the center of mass.

José explains these rounds with ease. "The first one was a tracer with a memory tag, and the second was an anti-armor 'tunneler' round. If you send that tracer in first, you can program all the other shots to follow. No matter which way the barrel is pointing." During this whole explanation, José is gesturing with his hands for emphasis. "And that 'tunneler' sucker—that thing can penetrate one-inch plate armor, burrow twenty more feet, and eliminate everything in a twenty-foot radius." He takes a deep breath. "That thing kicks ass."

The dark figure quickly squeezes off a four-round burst. José quickly tries to explain what each round of the burst is doing to the body. This becomes difficult, because there is not much left to the body after the acid and base rounds have transformed most of it into unrecognizable sludge. In the wake of this desecration, all that is identifiable is the left leg and the part of the right arm that had separated with José's first shot.

Leaving the S.Hi.T. rifle where it is, they all move back to the remaining tables to see what else is under the drop cloths. The last couple of tables do not have as much as the first tables, but they contain much larger equipment. The last item interests the dark figure, as José explains what the true function of it is—as well as its down side.

"Both of these are of equal power for thrust, but neither one has a warhead of any kind. I was not sure if they would be useful to you in this condition." José picks up the device and slowly spins it around, looking at it from all angles. He goes on, trying to entice his patron, "But seeing how there haven't been any more spider missiles on the market since that one group was stolen—I heard how effectively you had used them in the fighting around the Green Glass Zone—" José peers over toward the dark figure to hammer home the deal, "I thought I'd at least offer these to you," José says, finishing his presentation.

The dark figure looks over all of the tables, walking around each one, picking up some items and then placing them back down. Suddenly, the dark figure spins and asks, "How much? And what form of payment do you want?"

"The same form is always good. Five pounds uncut is more than enough—and rather fair, I think," José says with confidence.

The dark figure points to different items and says, "I will keep these items here in the City. The rest you will ship to the cause, and there you will be compensated with eight pounds uncut green glass. That should cover the complication of delivering them." Turning to José, the dark figure says gently, "Don't you agree?"

José smiles wide and shakes hands with the dark figure, finalizing the deal.

The spring wind blew in the fields, picking up the scents of the freshly cut winter wheat, budding flowers, weeds, and just good old fresh air, bringing these to the face of the driver. With only an occasional light cloud casting partial shadows in the fields, the sun shone brilliantly, causing shimmers in the road ahead. Freshly waxed red paint of the old SUV reflected the warmth of a spring sun back into the face of the driver. As local fence posts zipped by, the chortle of a few notes from a resting songbird could be discerned beyond the roar of the engine, and occasionally, an image of a red-winged blackbird blinked past. Reacting to the enthusiasm and thrill of the drive, the driver pressed harder on the gas, compelling the

SUV to travel even faster downhill into the rightward curve, so that more air flowed in through the four open windows. The SUV kicked up dust along the road, which then danced in swirling vortices in the rearview mirror. Traveling ever faster over the hills, the driver maintained impeccable control, even when traveling at speeds in excess of one hundred miles per hour.

Bang! Lighting is in the driver's eyes. Gone are the warm breezes and soothing aromas of the earth; the driver is no longer looking out of the SUV at times past. Now they are racing through the City, avoiding the traffic, chasing someone up ahead. Caught halfway between the heady memory and the present pursuit, the driver is unable to hear this world, except for the sounds of their own breathing reverberating through their body. The sounds of Remmington's yells are mute. The exact words she uses are a mystery, but the idea that attention must be paid to the other vehicle, which is getting away, is made clear with the look of panic on her face and by her hand gestures.

With a shake of their head, the driver refocuses on the perpetrators' vehicle and quickly skirts three vehicles that are crossing their path. Picking up speed, the driver can see that the end of the City is fast approaching and that the perpetrators are going to reach the end of the City in no time. Getting ever closer and still avoiding all the obstacles thrown in front of them, the driver is merely one block away, with a clear path between them and the perpetrators' vehicle, when the perpetrators reach the end of the City.

The perpetrators' vehicle speeds past the last buildings and plunges as if it were going off a cliff. Seconds later, the driver and Remmington are falling as well. Remmington's panic increases, and she braces herself, arms and legs stiff against anything she can reach, as both vehicles fall faster than rocks.

Remington is still screaming something, but silence occupies the driver's head. With time and space running out, the perpetrators' vehicle pulls out hard from the dive and kisses the ground, leaving a puff of sand, as they continue to race away from the City. The driver does the same, minus the kiss on the ground. The expert timing of this maneuver closes the gap between the two vehicles.

Now in the open, the pursuers can gain ground and close in even more. The accelerated speed pushes them back in their seats; Remington readjusts herself and regains composure. She pulls her targeting controls in front of her and prepares to disable the fleeing vehicle. This is complicated by the need to avoid not other vehicles but the occasional large saguaro cactus, craggy pinyon pines, and the multitude of different rock formations protruding from the ground. The purveyors of mayhem are trying to cross this inhospitable place, likely to seek refuge in the cliffs that lie beyond the desert.

Remmington's first disruptor shot is only a glancing blow and has no effect. After being hit, the perpetrators retaliate with small missiles from the back, giving the driver even more to avoid and thus providing the opportunity to prove why they are the driver. The new complications cause the second shot by Remmington to go wide to the left. On a straight run between some rock groupings, she lands a perfect hit.

It does nothing.

"Their systems are shielded. Get the Council to approve lethal force!" the driver instructs as they do a hop move over the latest salvo of missiles shooting at them.

Remmington wastes no time and is working on getting what the driver has requested, when the lights of the interior of their vehicle turn red and a warning message displays on the front window: WARNING! THIS VEHICLE WILL NOT OPERATE

OUTSIDE OF THE CITY LIMITS. TURN BACK NOW, OR THE
VEHICLE'S OPERATIONS WILL SHUT DOWN!

This message flashes five times and then turns into a graphical
display of a curved red line that stretches from one side of the
front window to the other side, with a model green vehicle
heading toward the line. As distances slip past under the
vehicle, the green icon ticks ever closer to the red line. With
one hand, the driver rotates the console Remmington is
working at and starts working on something other than just
getting approval from the Council. Remmington sits agape,
with nothing to do but watch events unfold.

The green model moves closer and closer to the red line.
Finally, the driver's controls in the vehicle start to change.
The top slips apart and seems to melt back into itself, as it
retracts to reveal the lethal firing controls. With a couple
more taps into the console from the driver, the vehicle's
transformation can be felt, along with a loss of speed, as
some of the aerodynamics of the vehicle are disrupted by the
deployment of the severe offensive weapons package. It is an
array of various warheads and delivery systems designed for
defensive and offensive engagements. Any remnants of panic
emanating from Remmington's face are now replaced with
shock, as she notes the readying of the lethal battery—even
though the Council still has not replied to her request for
lethal force approval. The array has positioned itself and is in
the process of entering launch data for each device; the final
authorization to send a weapon down range will come from
the driver.

Branches scrape along the side of the vehicle as the driver
maneuvers to avoid another volley of missiles from the
offenders. *I'm getting real tired of this game,* the driver thinks
as they line up a lethal shot.

The driver looses a battery of four missiles in rapid succession and two seconds later a second grouping of four missiles, so that all eight hit the other vehicle simultaneously. The maneuver of launching all eight missiles takes seven seconds. Five seconds after impact, the damaged vehicle is unrelenting and still racing toward the boundary line. As the pursued vehicle becomes unobtainable, the driver fires a third and fourth battery of missiles in the same way as the first two. This results in the perpetrators' vehicle becoming nothing more than a fireball, as it crashes into the ground, killing all the occupants and destroying the contents of the vehicle.

Quickly turning the vehicle to the right to remain in the operational zone, the driver runs along the City limits. Being right on the line causes power fluctuations in the lights and instruments until the completion of the turn away from the boundary. Slowing down, they make a long, sweeping arc back to the border to check the scene and confirm the destruction of the perpetrators and their cargo. After a quick scan allowing them to see the extent of the fire, the driver and Remmington return to Civil Central Command.

"Well, how are we going to fill out the order for the replacement of sixteen missiles when the Council never approved their use?" Remmington presses.

"Why, whatever do you mean? Approval?" the driver jokingly mocks as they exit the vehicle and head toward the lift. "Of course we *must* have had approval! How else could I've …" The driver makes an encouraging hand gesture for her to continue.

Remmington ignores the mockery. "Furthermore, how *were* we able to get fire control without their approval?" she asks in tones of anger, surprise, and awe.

The driver responds flatly, "The answer to both questions is the same."

Catching up to the driver in the lift, Remmington asks, "What, you hacked the system?"

The driver smiles coolly and asks rhetorically, "Did you think you are the only one who could hack the system?" They step off on the twenty-third floor. "We *must* have gotten the Council's approval. Or we will just have to change our reports as to how the perpetrators ended up as a bonfire on the edge of the City limits. Yes?"

Grabbing the driver's arm before they walk out of the front lobby, Remmington agrees, "Sure. Now what the hell was that at the beginning of the pursuit? You almost crashed. Where was your head?"

"My head was in driving," the driver answers in a very loose truth accompanied by a half smile.

"If you daydream like that again, you'll get us killed. I'm not one for dying just yet," Remmington says, teeth clenched, ending the conversation as she walks past the driver.

"Ben, what have you been able to recover?" the driver asks as the two of them wait for Remmington to return from her meeting with Cap and the Council.

Looking as nervous as ever, Ben answers, "After going over everything *twice*, I've found nothing." He shakes his head, "I'm surprised that it took the Council so long to start this investigation of the blackout, yet at the same time, now that they have, I'm afraid for my job, because it looks as if I'm going to be the scapegoat for this whole thing."

The driver soothes Ben's worries, "You heard the Cap. He's going to do his best to keep this off you, and with how bad this mess-up is, I can't see how they'll be able to pin it on you." They both turn toward the sound of an opening door.

Remmington comes in and joins the two of them, trying not to make eye contact with Ben until she takes a seat. She sits for a couple of seconds, with a worried look on her face, just staring into Ben's face and watching the sweat build on his brow. Ben is holding his breath and staring back at Remmington, nearly ready to pop.

"You're fine," Remmington finally says, cracking a smile. "This thing was way too big for any of the techs to say that you did it. So it's back to business," she exclaims and turns to the driver. "Now, you and I might have some trouble."

"Remmie, are you talking about the missile thing?" Ben asks.

Both the driver and Remmington shoot Ben a dirty look in an appeal to keep his mouth shut. Remmington tells the driver, "For now they don't seem to care, but one Council member did ask me about the miscount of missiles in the inventory."

The driver says, "They asked *me* that, as well. Come on, Remmie! You know how this works. They'll have to *zero* the balance sheets to cover up the discrepancy."

"So?" Remmington ventures.

"So the missing inventory will just *disappear*," the driver adds.

"That wouldn't happen," Ben interjects. "How would they account for the discrepancy in the credit transfers?"

"Look, they'll have well-placed bean counters just go back and—"

"Change the credits for each unit remaining," she finishes in a tone of awe. It is a lightbulb moment for Remmington as she utters these words out loud.

"I was going to say 'cook the books,' but that works, too," the driver comments.

"How do you know they'll do that?" Ben asks incredulously.

"Do you really think the system can get everything right—*all the time*?" the driver retorts. "Look, Ben, this is a bureaucracy we're talking about. Its existence depends on this sort of stuff." The driver turns toward Remmington, going back to the start of this tangent, "You know what, Remmie? I think they are asking all vehicle units about the miscount. Well, we can ask Cass; he sent me a message earlier saying he is coming up to talk to you."

"*Cac*, I forgot to turn my pager back on," Remmington swears as she pulls out her pager and turns it on. "I can't remember the last time he came up to the twenty-third floor. It must be something."

The driver props a leg on a lower drawer that is pulled out. Remmington pulls up something on her computer to read, and Ben pulls over a chair as they wait for Cassius Dorian to show up.

The rhythmic *tink* of metal against stone is apparent from as far away as the lifts. The distinctive sound of his metallic anatomy increases in volume as he enters the room.

"H-hello, Cassius," Ben stammers.

Cassius stops and looks at the young man. He strokes his soul patch for a moment with his natural arm. His eyes light up as he recalls his history with Ben. After his accident, Cassius was assigned office work, cold-case review, and he also helped with Ben's training. Ben tagged along and worked with Cassius on one case in particular, the case of a serial murderer. They did not solve the case but were able to determine that the murderer should be dead from old age at that point in the review.

"Aw, no way! Benny, it's been a while," Cassius says and shakes Ben's hand. He also gives Remmington a sly wink.

"Uh, so, Cass, what brings you up? You rarely come up here," Remmington asks.

"I actually just got back from a case. A man was found in a public restroom stall, dead, sitting on the toilet," he replies. "Two wounds were found in his legs. There was barely any blood at the scene. Weird, right?"

"Like Elvis?" the driver queries.

Cassius and Remmington turn and face the driver, bewildered.

"Who?" Remmington asks.

Ben fields the question. "Elvis was a singer in the ancient times," he explains. "Apparently, he was adored by millions."

"So, what, he had, like, a billion positive credits or something?" Cassius asks.

Ben gives him an incredulous look. "No, they didn't have credits in the ancient times," he says. "And he thinks he knows everything ..." he mutters as he rolls his eyes.

"So, wait. What does this Elvis guy have to do with the case?" Remmington asks the driver.

"Both Elvis and this guy died on the toilet. It's just a similarity," the driver says dismissively. "See, Elvis died of a drug overdose, and this guy was shot in the legs. The deaths aren't exactly the same, but the locations are," the driver finishes the random history lesson.

Ben tries to help out, "Well, if you think about it, it's kinda ... well, it's ..."

The bewildered looks of Remmington and Cassius transform into looks of astonishment, as both turn their gaze from the driver to Ben and then back to the driver, as Ben trails off.

"Never mind," the driver says, pushing past the awkward moment, and continues, "So, you say you found this guy in a toilet, but there was no blood? How's that possible? Didn't the blood spill out?"

"Nah, and that's the weird part," Cassius replies. "Apparently, all of the blood drained into the bowl. Processors are still looking it over, but that's what they came up with so far. These gunshots were measured perfectly for this sucker's legs. Damn near surgical precision, too—those two shots ripped through his femoral arteries, and while they were at it, broke the bones in his legs and stopped there. Poor *govniuk* couldn't get up, and it probably took all of five minutes for him to just bleed out."

Ben and Remmington simultaneously respond, "Seriously?"

"The screaming must have been horrendous," Ben observes.

"That's gotta be embarrassing! So, the victim is looking forward to a peaceful evacuation, sees this measuring rod, and then the next second, bam! He's hit and dying and stuck? That's crappy," Remmington finishes in almost a whisper.

They all have a little laugh at picturing how shitty a way this was to die. After a moment, Ben asks, "So, do we know who the victim is?"

Cassius explains, "Name's Gerry Colin. Occupation as a private security agent. Last time he was at work was four days ago. No one reported him missing 'til yesterday. Hell, the only reason we even found him was 'cause someone called in about the smell." He rubs his eye as if remembering the stench. "He was found in the SDN transport station bathroom, which isn't the best smelling as it is, so this must have been really rank. Anyway, the guy must've used it on his way home, 'cause no one would've been around to hear the shots or his screams, an' that station is usually packed. Colin got off his shift at 02:30, and according to his decomp, he's been there ever since."

Remington asks, "Any witnesses? Surveillance?"

Cassius continues, "Since a fuckton of people use that station, and since it's such a shithole to begin with, the scans will be completely useless to tell us who went in there. To top it off, SDN's security cams are all broken—have been for months."

"All of them? Why don't they fix 'em?" Ben inquires.

"S'pose some business uses the station as a place for backdoor deals, and they've been paying to keep it that way," Cassius directs his response to Ben before turning to the others to add, "And, get this: 'cause the stall was locked from the inside, the only lead we might have right now would be the rounds. They didn't even leave casings behind."

"So you have nothing to go off of, then?" the driver asks.

"As of right now, I can't see what they're going to come up with. I guess I'll start to try and run down the history of Gerry Colin and see where that leads me," Cassius answers.

Remmington wonders aloud, "Which security company did he work for?"

Quickly pulling up Gerry Colin's information on the computer, Ben speaks up first, "That's hard to say. Here, I have pulled up the pay transactions for one Gerry Colin, and there are four different accounts that have paid him in the past month."

"Yeah. Colin was a true merc. That's why I came to see ya, Remmie. Think you can get around the protection? See who was payin' him?" Cassius asks.

Remmington looks over Ben's shoulder to see the transactions. "Well, the third transaction on the list is not a security company. It's Red Inc.," Remmington says as she taps Ben on the upper back to get him to look at what she is indicating.

"Well, I'll ... G-squared! They are the only company that would pay such an odd amount." Ben pauses and then explains, "They're cheap. They use fractionals. See for yourselves," Ben says as he pulls back from the screen to allow the others to look.

Cassius gives Ben a curious look and asks, "How do you two know the pay rate of Red Inc.?"

Ben looks right back into Cassius's face and blinks purposefully twice.

Even the driver gets the hint and asks, "So how can we find out about the other three?"

Cassius smiles real big and, lacing his words with sarcasm, says, "Well, since we got this one down, think you two can do the follow-up for me? I mean, you *are* pretty tight with the company. I can check the other ones. Later."

Cassius gets up and gives Ben an affectionate rub on the head. Ben tries to whip his head out from under Cassius's hand like an offended child, but they are both smiling. Anyone can tell they are playing with each other. Cassius gives the driver a nod and extends his hand to Remington on his way out, saying, "Thanks again."

After Cassius walks out, Ben asks the other two, "So, he really didn't need our help?"

"Nope, totally screwing with us," Remmington quips. "Besides, everyone in the building knows your connections to Red Inc., Ben." Raising her eyebrows, Remmington prods, "That being the case, how about you take point on this for him—and because you took that shot at him when you were muttering something." She smiles.

Smiling at the ribbing from Remmington, Ben answers, "That's fine, but only because you two have so much other unfinished work." Ben needles them a bit, too. "You still haven't found anything related to the café crash, other than the name of Simon O. Larsen." It's clear by her body language that Ben is starting to get to Remmington. "And you still haven't identified what the cargo was in the chase that ended just outside of the City limits."

The driver decides to try to slow down Ben, who seems to be having too much fun, saying, "Well, that isn't totally truthful. If it had ended outside, we couldn't have returned without a tow from a transport vehicle." Taking the conversation in another direction, the driver continues, "Also, while you two had to go talk to the Cap and the Council, I finally got something on Simon O. Larsen."

Ben enthusiastically asks, "Why didn't you say something sooner? What did you find?"

"Yeah, what *did* you find?" Remmington queries, seemingly annoyed about being kept in the dark.

The driver answers casually, still having one leg resting on the open drawer, "I didn't want to repeat myself."

"Well, we are here now, so what did you find?" Remington repeats with some urgency.

"We were looking for someone whose vehicle would have been stolen or something, when we should have looked at the other detention centers' records, 'cause Simon has been in a couple of them. Never ours, and he has moved into different criminal outfits. The last detention center said to look into this arms dealer now, José Palmer," the driver finally shares the new information.

Remmington asks, "Why José? Is Simon that big of a criminal? 'Cause José is the biggest arms dealer at this point. The desert is probably fertile from all of the bodies José has put into the ground."

"So, if José is that bad of a guy, why is he still free?" the driver inquires.

Ben responds, "He knows the system." Remington nods in agreement. Ben continues, "For some reason, the evidence never puts him at the crimes. On top of these facts, witnesses won't speak up—or they end up dead."

"You're missing the part where some companies are paying to help protect him, 'cause he does a service for them." Remmington adds, "We just haven't figured out what. Yet."

"Remmie, are you still on about that case from three years ago that was thrown out?" Ben rebukes.

"I'm not 'still on.' Just pointing out that the Council member looking over the case was going to throw the book at him as her last act as a Council member—"

"Yeah, but—" Ben tries to interrupt, but Remington continues on without acknowledging him.

"*Because* she knew she had no way of winning her seat again. Then, two days after her *amazing* win, she dropped everything that was related to José's arms dealings," Remmington points out.

Ben sighs, clearly worn out with this part of the topic, and moves back to the matter at hand. "Why did they think Simon was working with José?"

"One of José's legitimate companies gave Simon a job, allowing for his early release from detention in the western jungle, the one close to Tixe Tower City," the driver tells them.

Remmington asks, "Did they give you a better address to try and locate him?"

"It was the same address that's in the system. The company that gave him the job is moving from one building to another, but they didn't say where *to* or even where *from*," the driver adds.

"Hey ... um ... you guys forgot to ask Cass about the missiles," Ben comments as he starts to go back to his desk.

Remmington grabs the closest thing at hand and throws it at Ben, hitting him with it. "Jerk!" she snorts under her breath. Laughing the rest of the way back to his desk, Ben ignores being hit with her pager.

"Come on, Remmie. Leave the kid alone. We've got work to do," the driver says flatly as they exit the office.

The Imp Club has lines of people outside waiting for a chance to get in. The three stories that the club takes up are only half of the floors that José Palmer owns in the Nolispe Tri Towers Number 3. They happen to be the only floors that Civil Central Command doesn't know he owns in this tower.

The bottom floor has a very open design; it is mostly used as a dance floor. Also on the first floor are one main crescent-shaped bar and two small bars in the far corners, opposite from the main bar. The second and third floors are open-air balconies overlooking the main dance floor. The second floor covers only three walls of the club. Over the crescent bar area is a stage that is not as high as the second floor but well above the first floor. It would be difficult, if not impossible, for the crowd to get on the stage from below. The third floor is reserved for private parties only. It has a perimeter of balconies with cross-walkways that lead to a circular dance floor over the very middle of the space below. The walkways jut from the corners of the balcony area, creating an *X* with a circle in the middle. The lighting effects play off the many different pieces of polished green glass, an opulence rarely seen. There is even a replica of an ancient disco ball, made out of green glass and suspended over the center of the dance floor of the private party level. The success of the Imp Club is in large part due to the pieces of green glass that adorn it throughout. This is a point not lost on José.

José sits down, wiping his brow and waving his hand for someone to get him a drink. *Dumb shit thinks the glass is here for him to take,* José thinks to himself as he reaches out for the drink. Looking at the limp body on the floor eight feet from him, José takes a sip of his drink and sets it on the table nearby. *I oughta fuckin' kill 'im.* He considers it for a moment. The breathing lump has been brought up to José by his security team, because the man was trying to chip a piece of green glass out of a door in one of the halls. To send a clear message, José broke the guy's jaw and nose before he passed out from the pain.

"All right, Matt! Remove him from my party. Go get him fixed up, and make sure the bills are paid for. Got it?" José barks at his security. "And get my guests back up here! We're celebrating a great pay day," he takes a gulp of his drink, which incorporates a piece of ice, "and the loss of Simon and what's-her-name." There is no real sadness in his tone as he mumbles their names around the ice in his mouth. "And may they be the last I lose to the cause this time," José adds as he lifts his drink and then drains his glass.

José's guests return with smiles and with no fear of José, even after witnessing the object of his retribution being dragged out. They have seen this vignette played out many times before. Some of them have had the initial misfortune of assuming the same starring role as the breathing lump. In their eyes, the man is better off this way. Some guests know that after José gets the man fixed up, he will be offered a job, so that he will not ever think or need to steal from José or anyone—at least, not anyone that is aligned with José.

This is how José built his power and has been able to maintain it. His power is not just attributable to the dark figure killing his old boss, Rachenov, promoting him. Nor is it because the dark figure only buys wares from José, giving José the most direct line to the expensive item, green glass. José hated Rachenov, but he knew that there were some of Rachenov's people who were very dangerous and would challenge his takeover. So he had to kill some of them because of how devoted they were to the horrible Rachenov. Yet, most acted like a pack of dogs, and after José beat them down, they fell into line. These many years later, only three of Rachenov's men still lived, and all three worked for José in some capacity.

Well after the disturbance to his party, José is in as deep a conversation as one can get with three women at one time. It finally slips into his conscious mind: the crowd is singing along with the song being played. Cold sweat comes at once, as the crowd sings: *"Bow down before the one you serve! You're going to get what you deserve! Bow down before the one you serve! You're going to get what you deserve!"*

José sits straight up and yells to one of his employees, "I said never play Nin!"

"God knows, money's not looking for the cure. God money's not concerned about the sick among the pure. God money let's go dancing on the backs of the bruised," the dark figure sings in perfect tune from a side table by themself.

That single voice with perfect pitch is the only one that pierces the noise of the club and paralyzes José. He is frozen in place as the rest of his guests then join in singing with the crowd, despite his objection. The dark figure stands up and joins José on the empty couch at the side of his sitting area.

Smiling, the dark figure says to José, "Mickey, it is surely all right if I play Nine Inch Nails?" Looking around the room at everyone who is singing, the dark figure remarks, "It makes me so happy to see how many followers you have with you these days, Mickey."

José swallows hard, "What did you call this?" José points his fat finger in the air, referring to the music.

"Oh. I said, it's surely all right if I play NIN?" the dark figure asks again. "You see, the true name of this ancient musical group is Nine Inch Nails. The archive data system was corrupted and shortened it to NIN, but no one knows the truth like your God. Now, isn't that right, Mickey?"

With the third occurrence of José being called "Mickey" by this stranger, some of José's guests stop singing. They look kind of crossly at the dark figure and then at José for not correcting this stranger. The look is all that any of them can muster, out of fear for what José might do for interrupting or correcting a guest of his, never mind what this unknown person might do.

As the song ends, José hoists his large frame off the couch, helps up the girls he's entertaining, and sends them to go somewhere else, giving the last one a kiss on the cheek as she gives his butt cheek a squeeze. After the girls have gone, José turns to find the dark figure standing right behind him with their arms open wide to give him an embrace. Although at first afraid of how close the dark figure is, José finally returns the embrace.

"Mickey, I know you have given up some people for me in the past, and once again at this time, but I am touched that you are finally seeing the value of the cause. I heard you tell Matt what this party was for," the dark figure whispers in José's ear as they embrace each other in this dangerous hug.

Stepping back and gesturing for the dark figure to sit again, José says, "I'm a little insulted. After twenty years of working with you, how could you think I wouldn't see the value of the cause?" *The truth is, the fact that you haven't changed in twenty years, and I don't want you to kill me as you did Rachenov,* José adds in his thoughts.

The dark figure rests back on the cushion of the couch and expresses, with some delight, "Mickey, I do believe that is the first time you have protested my actions ... What a good reason." They add in all seriousness, "Let's not make it a habit."

José starts to sweat again and asks, "Is there a problem? I heard where Simon's vehicle ended up."

"Things are going well. What you haven't heard about is the death of one Gerry Colin. That is mostly because I killed that infidel right before I came here," the dark figure grins triumphantly.

José responds with a slight shake of his head and a confused look, "Should I know who that is?" He searches the adjoining table for his drink, feigning nonchalance.

"A means to an end," the dark figure answers and then adds, "He lives by himself, and no one will report him missing for days. In that time, I need you to get someone to take over one of his security positions to steal a key card, so I can get into some labs." The dark figure leans closer to make sure José doesn't miss what is coming, "I think this is a fine way for some of your people to make up for the botched robbery, and I don't have the time to do it all."

"Which robbery are you talking about?" José asks apprehensively, fearful it was one he had nothing to do with the other day.

The dark figure looks upset by this ignorance and, with a wrinkled brow, says, "The one that ended just outside of the City limits. The one that headed straight for the ancient ruins, Mickey."

José's fears are confirmed and he concludes, *Yep, has to be one that I had nothing to do with.*

As if reading José's mind, the dark figure says, "I know you think that you had nothing to do with it. Don't even try to protest; it is all over your face." The dark figure leans back on one elbow, speaking patiently, "See, you need to look into the report again. It was the same group; I think they are called the Desert Fox or something. Weren't they the ones that stole the Spydertech Plura system for you and me all those years ago?" The dark figure wears a sly smile.

José's face turns red with anger, not at the purveyor of the information, but because he now understands why his attempts to contact the Desert Fox crew had failed. José had hired them to deliver the balance of the equipment that the dark figure had requested be shipped out of the City. He now understands why he hasn't been able to get hold of them. *Shit, they had half of the delivery with them,* José thinks.

Standing up, the dark figure says in parting, "Mickey, don't worry, I will give you more time to deliver my goods, 'cause I know you will deliver, and I'll still pay our agreed price."

José is thankful for at least that good news, as he watches the dark figure walk away. *I don't know how many times I have seen them actually leave the room. What, three times in twenty years?* José thinks to himself. Even before a signal can be given, Matt comes over with another drink for José.

"Matt, we need to find out what Gerry Colin looks like, immediately!" José growls, tipping the glass to his lips. "We need to know who we have that looks like him. Tonight!" He barks at Matt as he slams the rest of the drink.

Matt answers, "I will personally look into it." He takes the empty glass from José's hand. "At least no one's dead tonight."

"Why do you think you have to look up Mr. Colin?" José says, not interested in a response. He adds, "Find out what equipment we had packaged for delivery by the Desert Fox gang, and set it up to procure it all again, as fast as possible. Price is not an issue—just get it done fast! One more thing," José lowers his voice, requiring Matt to lower his head closer, "tell the bar to start watering down my guests' drinks."

The three of them stand outside Gerry Colin's rust-covered front door, waiting for the building's management company representative to show up with the different key cards to grant them entrance. This building is one of the latest attempts at government public housing. It was opened up to the public less than six years ago, and one third of the lights in the hallways have been damaged by the occupants and are still unrepaired. Any and all carpeting was removed from the public areas only two years after the opening.

This hallway only needs some dripping water, or water running down the walls, and this could be the set for a horror film, the driver thinks while listening to the pounding music emanating from the walls of Mr. Colin's place.

"How long did they say it was going to take to get someone here?" Remmington asks Cassius.

"This mother lode coming at you all three D's ..." The screaming vocals of the song are quite intelligible through the concrete walls.

Cassius shifts his weight and answers, "This is why I wasn't in a rush to get here. The management is damn near always slow to get on the scene with these kinds of places. Someone just had to be a speed demon, eh?" Cassius directs the last part at the driver.

"We got big news ..."

"Well, that wasn't all my doing. By the way, do you have my M.E. card, Remmie?" the driver asks her as she turns her back to them both.

"The band is kicking ..." The unrelenting music punctuates their conversations.

Cassius asks, "Remmie, did you place a bet on who would get here first?"

"and I see lots of beers ..." the song wails on as Remington swivels to look Cassius in the face.

"Yes to both of you. Here," Remmington says as she hands over an M.E. card to the driver. "And here we go," Remmington exclaims, pointing with a nod of her head at the short, skinny, long-haired old man walking down the hallway toward them, limping on his left leg.

"Sorry it took me so long, but we had to relocate all the neighbors of this unit because of noise complaints. The music has been playing like this for days, but since you say he's dead," his voice cracks, "he's not doing business here anymore, and I can let you into his property." Clearing his throat, the little old man continues, "I'd appreciate it if you'd take care of the music, now that I'm not breaking business laws by entering or letting you folks in. Oh yeah!" He starts to pull out seven key cards.

"Thank you for coming, Mr. Edgar. How are the knees?" Cassius asks, while taking some of the key cards to begin working on opening the door.

Mr. Edgar answers once he has handed over the last key card, "I have good days and bad ones." He pauses to consider the day, "Today is one of the bad ones. Well, I'm going to go. Drop the cards off when you're done. Thanks—and have fun with the music," Mr. Edgar says sarcastically before trailing off, mumbling something.

Cassius cracks the door and closes it again quickly. The heavy metal music's volume increases twofold when he breaks the seal of the door. Cassius says, "Okay, when I open the door, we got to shut that crap off, or we're gonna go deaf. Agreed?"

The others all nod their heads in agreement, and as soon as there is a break between songs, they race in to try to turn it off. Remmington finds the music computer first, sitting halfway into the room on a very messy desk. She tries to get around the locked screen, but is having no luck when the next song starts to play. She starts to yell something, but nobody can hear her over the excessive decibels filling the room.

Cassius is looking unsuccessfully at the utility panel across the room from the main door, trying to deduce which circuit would cut the power. Meanwhile, the driver walks to the oversized speakers and unplugs all of the cables from the back, one at a time. The last of the vibrations are still washing over the room as the cables dangle from the driver's triumphantly raised left hand.

"That's one way of doing it," Cassius drawls.

Remmington adds, "Yeah, it is, and now we know there's no damage to any of the evidence."

With the threat of hearing damage negated, the three of them start sifting through Mr. Colin's place. Remmington continues working on the pass code to look at the files on the deceased's computer. The other two move off into other rooms. Cassius peers into the closet next to the utility panel. The driver walks to the back of the place and tries one of the other four doors along the back wall.

The driver finds a basic restroom with a shower, a sink, and a toilet. The towel rack is halfway ripped out of the wall and has a medium-sized towel clinging to it for dear life. The floor is brown with grime or possibly a mélange of dried bodily fluids. The light for the room flickers on as the slow sensor takes stock of the driver's entrance.

At least this time it doesn't smell, the driver thinks thankfully.

Cassius finds mostly clothing in the closet, two locked briefcases, and a mix of plastic and steel storage boxes. He pulls everything from the closet and lays it all out to inventory the items. It becomes clear that the clothing is an array of different uniforms of various security groups or tactical undergarments. So there's a lot of black.

Cassius picks the lock of one of the briefcases to reveal three firearms: two pistols and one rifle, broken down into easily assembled pieces. Two clips for each weapon, fully loaded, are strapped onto the lid of the briefcase. Under the weapons' supportive material are the holster for the pistols and a strap for the rifle.

The second briefcase is full of M.E. cards and some credit-loading equipment. Cassius calls out, "Shit—if Colin's got all this, then why all the odd jobs?" He sits back with a sweep of his metallic arm, presenting his finds to the others. "I mean, even if these cards are only half-loaded, he could still afford a better hole than this."

"Maybe he didn't know what he had," Remmington speculates. "I just got into his computer, and it looks like some of the stuff he has listed here is unknown content." She scrolls further down the list, "And others have listings, like the weapons. Hey! Are there any numbers on those cases?"

As he searches the outsides of the cases, Cassius says, "No, but this looks like a bar code on the handle."

"Well, he has lists of personal and business holdings, with some numbering system for each," Remmington tells them.

The driver comments, "If the files aren't clear, it's going to take a while to catalogue all of this."

The lights that illuminate the gala are brighter than any in the night sky. They shine through the City so intensely that the driver's apartment glows even with its shades drawn. The driver waits anxiously for Remmington to show up at their doorstep. While looking in the fridge for the fifth time, deciding what to snack on, the driver hears the apartment's pager system go off. Engaging the intercom, the driver discovers that it is Ben who is at the other end.

"Hey! The Company lent me a luxury vehicle to ride to the event. I'm here to get you." Ben is quite energized.

"What about Remmie?" the driver asks over the intercom.

"She's leaving from the office, because she's working the event and needs to put on her uniform before she gets there," Ben replies.

"Be right out," the driver says, grabbing a pistol and heading out the door while securing the firearm on their person. In the parking area, two floors up from the driver's floor, sits an incredibly elongated vehicle. A massive Red Inc. insignia is splayed across the side panels. A nervous Ben is scanning the area. He is obviously in overprotective brother mode.

Sliding into the vehicle, the driver notices that a few other people are wearing the same attire as Ben. They all wear light-colored manila slacks and matching shirts that have short, straight collars and button up along the left side of the wearer. The sleeves have the Red Inc. insignia where buttons should be. The driver notices there are no pockets of any kind, either in the pants or on the shirt.

Sitting between these corresponding outfits is a gorgeous woman who absolutely stands out, and not just because of the uniformed look of the others. Her royal-blue evening gown wraps around her toned, tanned body, and a pear-shaped red diamond pendant accentuates her swan neck. She flashes a smile, revealing brilliant white teeth and dimples on either side of her petite nose. Ben takes his seat next to her and conducts his introductions while the vehicle begins its journey to the event.

"Well," Ben says, nearly stammering, "these four and myself all have received treatments." He indicates his compatriots by sweeping his open hand through the air.

The driver looks around, following Ben's hand, and notices that their eyes are distinguishable from normal humans'. The first subject to Ben's right has normal-looking eyes. The second subject, the only female, has violet eyes. Ben has those brilliant green ones. The fourth has red eyes. *It looks like the Red Inc. insignia for the irises,* the driver thinks. The fifth person has eyes with no pigment. It is almost as if they have a mirrored, polished look to them.

"Ahem," Ben clears his throat, "and this lady here is my sister, the artist Utionary."

The former "star" turns to her brother with a scowl, her auburn hair swinging around her face. "Please refrain from calling me that," she corrects. "You know I'm retired. Just call me Alice, Ben." Alice then turns to the driver and extends a hand in greeting.

"Just to let you know, folks, we'll be arriving shortly," informs the vehicle operator. The five then don sunglasses as the finishing touch to their outfits, for they are to be on exhibit.

"Can you actually see in those things?" the driver queries.

"You'll understand more when we get inside and begin our presentation," one of the men replies.

The driver is looking out the window at the crowd and can't tell which one of the passengers said this but thinks it was most likely the red-eyed one. The vehicle pulls into a procession and waits to unload its passengers.

When the vehicle finally reaches the destination, the driver exits the vehicle and scans the area for possible threats. They then motion for Alice to come out. Alice gives her brother a hug and a peck on the cheek, wishes him luck, and steps out of the vehicle. The crowd held at bay cheers as she fully unfolds from the vehicle. Ben stays inside with the rest, as they are to be deposited at an employee entrance. The driver steps back and gives the former artist space, as she welcomes the mixed responses of screams and boos. It could be compared to a sports team arriving on the field, with cheers and jeers filling the air. This din only heightens the driver's sense of awareness.

A large, crazed fan, or possibly a fanatic, tries to push his way through the crowd. The security detail is on him like a bolt of lightning. By the time the driver becomes aware of this man rushing toward their escort, the fan has already been tackled and hog-tied.

Ben didn't need me or anyone else to escort his sister, the driver thinks while moving Alice toward the building's lobby and greeting area.

Walking up the stairs to the door, the driver sees one of the vehicles from the Civil Central Command making another pass around the event. At the door, Alice presents the pass for herself and the driver. Once inside, they see seven different lines of guests waiting to be scanned. Working the line second to the right end is Aly. The driver guides Alice toward Aly's line, because it happens to be the shortest at that moment.

"So does this mean that Ben is here?" Aly asks the driver.

Alice responds with her own question, "You must be Aly? Hello, I'm Benjamin's sister, Alice."

"Yes, I am. It's nice to finally meet you. I really *hate* your music. I gave you thirty credits," Aly concludes succinctly with a twinkle in her eye and an unmistakably warm, truly friendly smile.

Alice looks pleased with this and says, while taking Aly's hand and shaking it, "Thank you so much. Do you want any of that back? 'Cause I think I have an M.E. card in my handbag, here." Alice opens her bag up and starts to pull out an M.E. card.

Lifting her hands up, palms facing forward, and shaking her head, Aly interrupts. "No, no. You earned it. Besides, I have gotten more than that out of Ben," she giggles, "with the dinners he's bought me." Aly smiles and winks at Alice knowingly, causing the two of them to laugh at a secret known only to them.

After their laughter dies down, Aly scans Alice first, getting a green light to enter. While she is scanning the driver, the alarm goes off, giving them a red light because of their sidearm. Aly quickly enters a code into the scanner, and the driver's reading turns from red to green. The driver nods thankfully to Aly; there are whispers about what just transpired as they move to join Alice again.

"So, did Ben ask you to take this so seriously, or do you always travel with a weapon?" Alice asks. The back of her left hand is on her hip, holding her handbag, while her right removes a flute of some bubbling drink from a passing server's tray.

The driver picks up a glass as well but doesn't drink out of it and says, "Ben asked me to keep you safe, and seeing as I would've been working security no matter what, I might as well be prepared."

"I see. Well, let's go mingle. I'm sure there'll be something interesting to see." Alice takes a sip of her drink. "There are three different companies displaying products here tonight," Alice says, turning and waiting for the driver to walk next to her. "This should be fun." She laughs as they move into the main mass of people.

Quickly the driver observes how fame is an encumbrance and that Alice has to deal with its burden—more so because of her beauty. The two of them never take more than one step before someone stops them to talk with Alice. Some people give the same kind of comments that Aly had about hating Alice's music, while still being very polite and excited to meet her. Others ask if she would be willing to do appearances for them. *She's definitely a celebrity,* the driver thinks. Most of the people pay no mind to the driver. Only the Council members engage the driver, yet they engage everyone, so as not to offend the host companies.

Politicians are always trying to kiss the babies, the driver ruminates as they stand by Alice, trying not to look too bored.

Forty-seven minutes into the event, people are still arriving, and the expositions aren't scheduled to start for another thirty minutes. The people in the crowd settle into comfortable conversations and act as if they could care less for anything more to happen. Alice and the driver find a spot to stand and let the crowd rotate around them, as they talk to a Dr. Logan Rea.

Dr. Logan Rea is not the tallest man, but by no means is he a short man. His light-brown, very well-groomed, medium-length full hair; his impressive brown eyes; and his solid body provide Dr. Rea with the raw material to hold the eye of any woman at the gala.

Dr. Rea had stopped working for Red Inc. just after Ben started the negotiations for his eyes. So Alice and Dr. Rea had met back then and are now talking about what they have been up to in the interim. This leaves the driver with limited opportunities to contribute to their conversation. Fortunately, Remmington finds them.

"Alice. You look amazing," Remmington says as they hug in greeting.

Smiling, Alice says, "Well, you're looking really good yourself. I could never look that good in that uniform, whereas you could totally pull off this dress," Alice laughs, making a sweeping motion with her hands across her own gown for emphasis. She continues, "Remmie, this is Dr. Logan Rea. For a short time he was one of Ben's doctors, before he moved on to start working on—genome mapping—or DNA—I'm sorry. I missed what you said you were doing with the DNA."

"Well, my dear, that is because I never said what I was doing with it," Dr. Rea says with a little laugh.

Alice scolds him with a girlish pout, "Well, Logan, that's not fair! Withholding things and then leaving me to stand here drowning like that." The two of them laugh at some private joke that is laced into Alice's playful response. Remmington and the driver are both lost as to what the joke could have been.

"How is your day going?" the driver turns to Remmington and asks, freeing Alice and Dr. Rea to continue their private joke without explanation.

"Well, I was late, and the Cap wasn't happy about that, because he gave me a ride," Remmington answers. "But it turns out it was good we were late, 'cause as soon as we showed up, some crazed fan tried running for Alice," Remmington adds, gesturing toward the famed musician.

The driver asks, "So you saw that? Was it you who took the guy down?"

Looking a bit disappointed and surprised, Remmington answers, "No, the Cap totally took that guy down all by himself. I helped haul the guy away, but the Cap did it on his own. All I said was *there!* and he was on the guy in a blink of an eye. It's those long legs of his."

"Well, I wasn't always in charge, Remmie," the Cap's voice booms as he approaches the two of them from the side.

Remmington leans into the driver and whispers, "It's the damnedest thing! He's old, but he hears everything." The driver smiles knowingly.

"I did hold your position a long time ago," the Cap grins at Remmington. "Alice, you look beautiful tonight. And Dr. Rea, I hope your presentation is as entertaining as the last one I saw of yours." He shakes the doctor's hand vigorously.

"I don't know about that; which presentation was it that you saw?" Dr. Rea asks as the two men turn and continue their talk.

This leaves Alice to join the conversation with the driver and Remmington. The small talk continues until both the Cap and Remmington simultaneously stop talking in midsentence.

The gala's opulent dome is easy to see from the perch where the dark figure set up the S.Hi.T. rifle. The dark figure has one clip loaded and one ammo box full of belted rounds immersed in an oil. Setting up the angle took less time than the dark figure had allotted. *Well, if the fool wishes to stand in the same place the whole night, who am I to fight my will?* the dark figure pontificates as they load the clip into the rifle.

The dark figure fires the first round, just as it happened in the warehouse. The round—the special round—hits the window between the dark figure and their target, without breaking the pane. Instead, the round breaks apart when it hits and oozes its core contents onto the barrier. The encapsulated cargo transforms the window pane, essentially dissolving it into dust. Pleased with the alignment of the shot, the dark figure unloads the clip onto the same pane, hitting near the top so gravity will spread the core ooze. With the clip spent, the dark figure removes it and adjusts the receiver of the rifle to uptake the belted rounds.

"Remmie, I'll look into it. Someone may have opened a vent in the dome to prevent it from getting stuffy in here," Cap says, then turns and leaves to investigate the radio report that interrupted both of them in midsentence.

Alice starts grilling Remmington, "Remmie, what message did you just get?"

Doing her best to diffuse the stress in Alice's voice and the look on Dr. Rea's face, Remmington says with confidence, "It's just as the Cap said. Someone opened a vent to let out some of this heat." She turns away quickly to hide her own doubts and begins scanning for discrepancies.

The adjustments finished, the dark figure looks right at the target through the scope, the glass eaten away by the acid-ooze rounds. While still sighting the target in the scope, they open the ammo box but stop before pulling the end of the belt out, in order to make one final adjustment to the scope. Still vigilantly keeping their target in the scope, the dark figure loads the belt with well-rehearsed actions.

Not relieved by Remmington's reassurance, the four of them scan the perimeter walls to see if they can locate the vent controls. Distracted, they pay little attention to the Council member who has returned to hobnob with Alice again—when Dr. Rea falls to the ground with a grunt and grabs at his abdomen.

Remmington tackles the Council member, shielding his body with hers, and pulls her weapon once she has the Council member protected. Driver does the same with Alice. Dr. Rea screams with pain, but there is no blood on the ground and only a small discoloration on his shirt, which is making it difficult to tell whether he really has been shot. Everyone else starts to panic and move away, since there are five people on the floor for unknown reasons. While covering the Council member and Alice, Remmington and driver share looks of confusion.

Looking at Remmington, then at Dr. Rea, who is screaming even louder, and back at Remmington, driver says, "Is he hit? Either way, we need to get these two out of here!" Driver scans the room, trying to determine the direction of the potential threat.

"I don't know. You get them out of here. I will che—" Remmington stops in midword, watching the doctor's clothing jump, as more rounds slam into his body. The subsequent rapid ballooning of Dr. Rea's body is unmistakable to driver.

"He's going to explode! Get back! MOVE!" driver shouts.

Scrambling away from Dr. Logan Rea, the four of them only get a few steps before he violently erupts, dispensing pieces of himself up to twenty feet into the crowd. Pieces of rib bone hit the people still within eight feet. The nearly silent explosion cannot be heard over the sounds of the fleeing crowd, and the people farthest away are calmed. All they can ascertain is that someone's screaming has ended. Hysteria ripples out from the epicenter as the crowd becomes aware of the gore that has spread from what used to be a person.

Remmington and driver quickly check the Council member and Alice to find they are unhurt and relatively clean, because both of them were shielded by the two civil servants at the time of the bombardment. Remmington and driver are not as unscathed by the doctor's remnants.

"You have a bit ..." Alice gags a little. "There's a bone in your pant leg, Remmie." She points at the bone fragment.

"No, that's actually *in* my leg. And you're bleeding from your neck," Remmington says to driver as she grabs a napkin to cover the cut in the back of driver's neck. Then Remmington seems to talk to herself, "Tell Ben his sister is fine. We need to get everyone out of here before more shooting continues. So far, no one else has been shot. The collateral damage seems minimal; body parts from the victim have injured some of the guests."

Driver guides the Council member and Alice towards a side wall and says, "Let's make sure we are out of the line of fire."

Limping along, Remmington asks, "Are you sure this is the way the shots came from?"

"What? We are going toward the shooter?!" the Council member says in a panic and begins to struggle, attempting to travel in a different direction.

"No. We are *not* going in the wrong direction," driver responds to the Council member and then to Remmington, "And, yes, this is the direction I determined from how the doctor's clothing was jumping." *And if I was wrong, we would still be getting shot at.*

Alice grabs the other arm of the Council member to assist driver in keeping the group moving to safety.

Driver reassures everyone as they reach the outside wall, "The wall here will cut down on the angle of their shots and give us cover."

Talking to herself again, Remmington says, "Cass, do you have eyes on where the shots came from? ... Cap, do we know which vent was opened? ... Cass, try focusing on the west side; I repeat, *west* side."

"Was I right?" driver asks over the pandemonium of the crowd.

"I have no idea. None of the vents are open. It's a better hunch than nothing," Remmington answers as she and driver stand guard over their charges.

The rifle jumps for the last time as the belt is fully spent; dark figure doesn't even check to see if the good doctor is going to expire or not. Instead, dark figure efficiently sanitizes the shooting area and is on the move by the time Cassius makes his first pass. Unlike at the café, dark figure leaves no personal physical evidence.

No need for them to start to see more of a pattern, dark figure surmises.

Remmington, Ben, and driver sit in the Cap's office, waiting. All three of them wear heavy protection suits, with the protective face guards and helmets off. These black uniforms are made of overlapping scale-shaped plates of ballistic-resistant material that shine like the vehicles down in the launch center. The overlapping design of the suits gives protection from not only firearms but also stabbing and slashing weapons. The padding of these uniforms helps protect against concussive blasts. A down side to these uniforms is that the bulk makes the wearer less agile, and the padding can cause the occupant to overheat.

From the side door next to the couch, the Cap walks in, waving them to remain seated as they start to stand, according to protocol.

Cap jumps right into it and preempts any questions by announcing, "The Council is not pleased with this assassination." Cap rubs the back of his neck, "But thank God you two were there to protect the one Council member and the high-value guest, your sister, Ben. If anyone else had been critically hurt or killed, I don't think I would still be standing here." He begins to pace slowly.

"Red Inc. is not calling for my removal or termination," Cap continues, "but Dr. Rea's new employer is, and the third company at the gala is currently abstaining from any such request." He stops and faces the three squarely, "As long as they withhold their option to remove me, I'll be here. Now it will be up to us to keep me here. 'Cause, let's face facts, if they walk me out, you guys could be out with me. To add more to this mound of shit, the Council has called into question the security preparations for the upcoming holiday. M.P. Day is the most important holiday to the Council; since this is the basis for their seat of power, they like everyone to embrace it fully. So, tell me what you have."

Driver stands up, "We should move to a conference room, so I can display some information and add in Cass and maybe Aly, too."

"Lead the way," Remmington says.

As they are all walking out, Ben asks, breathing a little hard and sweating, "Cap, can we take off the heavy uniforms?"

"Not until this assassin is taken down. My order for these uniforms stands," Cap barks at Ben's whining.

The conference room is an oval room with the ends cut off. There is a door in the middle of each of the two curved walls. The walls have maps and other graphics projected onto them, everywhere except where the doors are. The table in the middle of the room is an elongated trapezoid shape that seats eleven, so whoever presents can see every face with ease as they stand at the wider end.

Driver takes this space as everyone enters the room. The Cap takes the far end of the table, sitting on the narrow end of the trapezoid, which is just wide enough for one person. Remmington walks around the table, while Ben sits at the closest seat and immediately starts to work on the tablet at that location, trying to lower the room temperature.

Driver turns off all the existing graphics projected on the long walls and starts to bring up different graphics, then establishes a video conference link with Cassius and pulls up a blank video conference screen that is intended for Aly.

"We have learned who all of the five victims of the café crash were. The two that the vehicle hit first and instantaneously killed worked directly with Dr. Logan Rea." The wall space behind driver has lists of events and names. As driver talks, each item shows up, and lines appear between names and events.

Events:	Victims:
Café Crash	Five people killed
SDN Station Murder	Gerry Colin
Gala Assassination	Dr. Logan Rea

"This is possibly why their company is looking to have you removed, sir, since employees have been dropping, and they don't see all we're doing. Other than this fact, these deaths have no clear relations. Cassius has a theory for some other connections. Cass?"

Cassius's screen switches places with the graphic of lists as he begins talking. "It's possible Gerry Colin was killed 'cause one of the companies he worked for had consulted for the gala. Colin wasn't on the roster for security, but it's possible that he had access to a guest list as well as information on which areas were covered by specific security details."

The Cap interrupts, "Are you all saying that there is no such thing as coincidences?" They all turn their attention toward Cap. "Do we have a killer with some kind of grudge or vendetta with this one company on our hands?"

Remmington takes over at this point. "We have a number of different victims and only one lead on the aggressor in any of these cases: Simon O. Larsen. With the blackout and computer error, we are just now learning where Mr. Larsen was working. He worked as a janitor in a building that is being remodeled by one of José Palmer's construction companies. There hasn't been anyone at this building working on it for weeks, and the reasoning behind this absence is unclear. Council just gave us approval to search this building to see what evidence we can find."

Remmington pauses as Aly appears in her screen. "Hello, everyone. Sorry for being late," Aly hails.

"You've got perfect timing. I just finished. What've you got?" Remmington responds.

Aly's screen is transferred to the main display, and she begins her report. "I just found and finished processing what I believe is the shooting nest for the gala assassination. The scans put this spot at a 99.89% probability for being the place, based on the angle between Dr. Rea's body and the window. The only issue is that there is nothing here that can really prove that a S.Hi.T. rifle was used or who the shooter was."

"Who said anything about a S.Hi.T. rifle?" the Cap asks with concern and interest in his voice.

Remmington speaks up again, "I was going to make that link. The connection comes from the evidence on Dr. Rea's body and the missing pane in the dome. Aly, would you please fill in what you found from these two areas for this scene?"

"Sorry for jumping the gun, Remmie. There weren't any pieces from the missing window found, but in the scans of the gala floor, there were irregular levels of—"

Cap inquires for clarification, "Back up. If the window is missing, how can there be no broken pieces? And why would the assassin need to remove the window pane before taking the shot? It seems to me that this was an excessively complicated murder."

Aly attempts to answer, "It is probable that the window was eaten away to give the assassin a clear shot at Dr. Rea. After it was silently removed, the shooter would have ample time to change the type of ammunition used for the actual assassination. Collecting the remaining pieces of Dr. Rea and searching for nonbiological items showed an abnormal amount of a special type of oil. This oil is only used in a couple of places, and unless Dr. Rea had been drinking it, the oil had to be introduced into his body from the rounds that hit him. Rounds containing sodium would be stored in special oil so that they would not interact with the water in the air. *Sodium* is what caused Dr. Rea to expand and ultimately explode. In order to introduce that much sodium rapidly into a person, the rounds must have been belted.

"These two pieces of evidence, combined with the limited space constraints in the probable shooting nest, has led me to theorize that the weapon had to be a S.Hi.T. rifle. It's the only rifle that could shoot both a round to render the window pane ineffective and then rather quickly shoot belt-fed sodium rounds in such a confined space.

"Now, José Palmer is suspected of having a cache of the older model rifles, and with Remmington's input, I do believe he now has the improved S.Hi.T. rifle—the older model couldn't handle belt feeding," Aly says to complete her report. She switches her screen with the first graphic screen again.

Driver and Remmington sit down and look to Cap. Throughout the briefing he has been twisting the dark-gray band on his finger and is now in deep thought, still doing this as everyone waits for his thoughts and orders. A couple of times he removes the band, flips it over, and puts it back on again.

Flipping the band and giving it a twist, the Cap says, "Cass, have you tracked down all of the companies Mr. Colin worked for yet? We need to see if José has any more ties to his murder, 'cause what you have here is too weak to link José or his outfit to the Colin murder.

"Aly, I want you to find out everything you can about that oil. Who makes it, who uses it, and if there was any other way of it getting into Dr. Rea's body. And triple-check to make sure this oil was really part of his remains and not part of the scene or a contaminant or something like that.

"Ben, the Council has determined that you had nothing to do with the blackout. We would like you to start looking into rebuilding the graphics of the crash from the witnesses' reports. Seeing how the cleanup crew cleaned up the café and vehicle before we could get back to redo the scans, you will have nothing else to go off of—sorry. Aly, give him any help he might need with this, please. Ben, please try to focus on where the ACC was removed and where the operator of the vehicle got out."

"Yes, sir," Ben and Aly respond in unison.

Cap continues, "As for you two, you have your orders from the Council to look into the life of Simon O. Larsen. I want to know everything about him ever since he got here and why we haven't gotten any flags for a missing person from his work yet. I don't care whose arms you have to twist—just get it done. We're behind on whatever is going on here, and we are running out of time. This trail is getting cold."

As they pull their vehicle into the ground-level lot, driver and Remmington notice that Gamma Pharmaceutics' new sign is almost completely mounted on the side of the building—except for a few missing letters. Many floors of the building are open to the outside environment, because they are still under construction. The lot is barren of any workers or vehicles. Other than a couple of construction lifts that look like they have not been moved in some time, there is nothing in the lot. The light of the noonday sun glints off the exposed steel and glass of the structure, almost blinding the two as they approach.

"Doesn't look like there are any arms here for us to twist," Remmington says with a smile.

Driver smirks. "Yeah, right."

"And you know what? No people means no trash to take out—Simon must've had an easy time janitoring here," Remmington rolls her eyes as she says this.

The lowest level is enclosed, but none of the doors are locked. The two of them walk right in to see the information and front security desk without occupants behind it. Looking over the top of the desk, Remmington can see that the computers are on and unlocked.

"Weird," driver says as Remmington points to the screens and moves around the desk to get a better angle to read them.

"Gotta love the hired help," Remmington says playfully to driver.

Driver walks away, calling over their shoulder, "I'm going to check and see if anyone is in the restroom."

Remmington answers back as she starts to work on the computer, "Good idea. Don't forget to check them both."

Driver checks not only the restrooms but also every door and pathway that is accessible without brute force. After picking a lock to a gate, driver gains access to a path to get back to Remmington without backtracking. Walking up behind Remmington unnoticed, they give her a bit of a scare. Remmington spins around, her weapon drawn and trained on driver.

"G2. How did you come from that way?" She quickly points her weapon to the floor. "I saw you on the monitors, but the computer says that gate is locked," Remmington huffs as she puts away her weapon.

Driver gives her a bemused smile and says, "I picked it so I didn't have to double back. What has you so jumpy? What if I was the guard to this place, or something?" Driver's comments fall on deaf ears.

Remmington refocuses her attention on the screens in front of her for a moment, before saying, "Not all of the systems are up and running in this building." The screen has a graphic of what looks to be floor plans, but in a three-dimensional layout, with layers of floors transparent through other floors. As she touches the screen with her finger, she can move the view from layer to layer, in any direction, on any axis. She scrolls through the building and continues to explain her findings, "The one system that is online is the body system— the one used in case of a fire to see if someone is still alive. Well, the system shows there are some *things* in the building." Her emphasis on the word *things* is enough to pique driver's interest.

"Please clarify what you mean by 'some *things*'?" driver asks suspiciously.

Remmington taps on the screen to direct driver's attention to the red lights. Not being made any wiser by Remmington's gesture, driver looks at the screen, puzzled, and then back at Remington, as she turns quickly and walks to the lifts.

"I have no idea," she calls back and checks that her weapon is clear. "The system lists them as organic heat signatures, and the video feed for the building isn't available." Driver moves quickly to catch up with her. She is still several paces ahead as she continues, "I also found a shipping invoice for a bunch of weird stuff. I don't really know what it was, and I don't want to."

They continue their way to the lift; driver also checks that their weapon is clear. Remmington pushes the button to go up. A few moments pass by as they wait for the lift, before driver inquires, "Which floor are we going to?"

"The CEO's office. Mr. Carwrite is on the seventeenth floor, according to the building's manifest. Maybe we can find some more information there," Remmington replies as the lift doors open.

Stepping off the lift, driver begins to think of the different crime scenes. *Why nurses? What could they have done to—*

This line of thinking is cut off as driver falls and plunges into deep darkness. The deadened *thud* of a corpse and the accompanying groan can be heard through the darkness. Driver lands on their back with a brief jolt of pain, staring at the hole they came through. Groaning from the hard landing, driver gets up and tries to make sense of what happened.

"Oy! You okay?" Remmington asks from way above.

Driver looks up to see Remmington peering over the open hole. "Yeah, I broke my own fall," driver jokes back, while still trying to work out the stinging pain.

"What's down there? How did you do that?" Remmington calls down. Driver can tell she is finding the event funny. "Do I need to get some rope or come down there to help you?" Remmington asks as she rustles through some stuff on the floor above.

Looking around, driver responds, "Dunno what is down here. I can't see much. There are no lights, but I should be able to find my way out of here. Maybe take some stairs if I can find 'em."

Still trying to let their eyes adjust to the darkness, driver hears a snarling sound, somewhere in the blackness to the left. Driver spins in the darkness, pistol already drawn. Another growl joins the snarl.

Christ, driver curses in their head. *What a ruddy beautiful day—*

This thought is interrupted as one of the snarling things slams into them and passes back into the darkness. The body knocks driver far back from the hole and to the ground. As driver falls and hits the ground, their weapon discharges, sparking an explosion of pressurized gas tanks that blows out part of the outside wall. Fire ignites one of the creatures and some of the surrounding construction material. The hole in the exterior wall and the small flames illuminate the area around the now-burning, snarling thing.

"Remmie! Classification of 'things' is correct! Good job—" driver shares. *G2!*

The creature stands on four legs and is three feet tall at the front shoulders. The front shoulders are oversized and bulging with well-defined muscle. It has short, dark-brown to black fur and no real tail of any length. As it turns, driver notices that its face has a snub nose and plenty of mean-looking teeth. *Definitely made for ripping and tearing flesh.* It growls in obvious anger and pain at driver.

Driver lifts their weapon and shoots the beast right before it charges at them, hitting it twice and dropping it dead.

"What the hell is going on down there?!" Remmington yells in a concerned voice.

Before driver can answer or find the other creature, it slams into them again. This time the beast not only knocks driver to the ground but almost out of the hole from the explosion. If the beast hadn't landed on top of driver, they would have gone sailing sixteen floors to the ground. Instead, the concussive force of the beast landing on top of driver causes their weapon to take the sailing trip.

"Remmington!" driver yells, trying to hold the beast's head away from biting theirs, thinking, *This is one ugly giant pug dog!*

Remington hears driver's struggle outside the building and opens a nearby window to look down the side of the building.

"What the hell is that?" Remmington exclaims as she looks down at the back of the giant pug's head.

"Does that really matter right now? It has me pinned, and I killed its friend." Driver struggles to stay out of its snapping jaws. The thrashing of the animal makes it hard to explain everything. "I need your weapon. Aaaaa!" driver yells in pain, as the animal starts to rake its hind legs across driver's body, ripping some of the protective scales off.

Dispensing with further questioning, Remmington pulls out her weapon and tries to line up the drop to the one free hand driver has. With no count, Remmington just says, "Here," as she drops it to her partner. The weapon spins in the air, and the rotation of the spin causes it to pass driver's fingertips without touching. As the weapon passes into memory, both partners utter an audible groan.

"Remmie!" driver screams up in frustration and desperation as the giant pug dog snarls and snaps ever closer and rips another scale off. Remmington quickly has her backup weapon in hand and drops it so it doesn't spin as it falls. As it lands solidly in the palm of driver's hand, they wrap their fingers around the grip. Just as the animal removes another scale and makes a large enough hole in the uniform to expose driver to an open attack, driver places the weapon up against the giant dog's head and pulls the trigger. From the force of the weapon being pushed up against its head and the following shot, it rolls dead off driver.

Continuing with the recoil from the weapon, driver rolls in the opposite direction, ending up on all fours, looking out of the hole in the wall toward the ground. Breathing heavily, driver calls out, "Nice drop. Thank you. We should go find our weapons before something else happens."

"Yeah, good idea. I'll meet you at the lift—hey! Who's down there by the vehicle?" Remmington asks as she looks past driver toward the ground. Driver also focuses on the movement below. Without another word, they both disappear into their respective openings and scramble to get back down to the ground level.

Emerging from the lift, driver and Remmington can see the front of their vehicle and someone running away. The distance and speed of this individual make it difficult to discern any identifiers as to whom they are. The suspicious character then jumps into a different vehicle and takes off. Their vehicle's doors open as Remmington and driver run up to it and dive in. The other vehicle's lead is significant, but with the skill of driver and the power of their vehicle, they quickly start to close in on the suspect.

"Just give me a clean shot, and I'll have him," Remmington says as she starts to power up the disruptor.

Driver glances at Remmington out of the corner of their eye and says, "Don't worry, I'll get you close so you can hit her."

Remmington pauses what she's doing with the disruptor to look at driver. She's about to debate the gender contradiction, when a warning message displays across the front window.

WARNING: FOREIGN OBJECT DETECTED. ACCELERANT DETECTED. VACATE FOR SAFETY.

The automated voice system calls out the warning to gain the occupants' attention. After flashing the warning twice, a schematic of the side profile of the vehicle appears, with the lower back highlighted red to indicate where the foreign objects are located.

"Remmie, just tag them! We don't have time," driver says, just as a rumbling sound is heard behind them.

Remmington switches the controls to a tracking dart and as she shoots to tag the vehicle, the world flips end over end. Rockets with no warheads continue until their fuel is depleted. Luckily, driver is able to send their vehicle down a straight path between the buildings. After the third flip, the vehicle they are chasing is lost in the mess of traffic.

"He is in a foul mood."

"The CEO is up his ass about the other programs."

"Well, I hardly see why that is our fault. So many people have died working on that program."

"Killed. They were *killed!*"

"Still, not our program. We are doing some good work here, and he just tried to rip my head off. He is such an asshole." The couple steps out of the small room. She buttons the last button on her yellow blouse, turns to him, and says, "I will have to go back to his office now with my report. The one you're stepping on."

"Carol, it'll be all right. Here," he reassures her while picking up her report tablet and handing it to her.

As she takes the report, she puts her arms around his neck,

giving him a quick kiss, and says, "Will it be all right? I think it is all right now." She teases him with another quick kiss.

They quickly break apart, startled, as they hear another door down the hallway open up. They see one of the interns step out, pushing a closed, locked cart.

"Hello, Zenas," Carol calls out. Zenas is one of the three interns, easily identified by his rare platinum-blond hair. The status as an intern is made clear by the white lab coat and his young age.

Zenas ensures the door is closed behind him and turns to answer her greeting, "Hello, Miss Tuttle and Mr. Risk. I will have the lab locked down before the end of the day, and it looks like everything is accounted for, so far."

Mr. Risk asks suspiciously, "What are you talking about? Why is that lab being locked down?"

Carol ignores his questions and asks Zenas her own instead. "Are you doing the lockdown by yourself? Where are the other two? I thought he gave all three of you the task of locking down that lab until they find out what happened this weekend with the break-in."

Standing behind his cart, Zenas looks down at it and answers, sounding slightly hurt, "Well, with the murder of Dr. Rea ... Beth was involved with him and was very upset to be here. Nic took her out to try—" Zenas cuts off his own words.

"Dr. Rea was sleeping with her, as well?" Carol remarks with shock and maybe a bit of jealousy.

Mr. Risk raises an eyebrow to Carol and says to Zenas, "So, how does a weasel like Nic get a girl like that to agree to go out with him?"

Zenas says, choking on his words, "Nic ... he's a nice guy."

Finally collecting herself, Carol says, "That's shit. Zenas, you're way better than Nic. He is a weasel—he's such a smartass. I want to smack the crap out of him half the time."

"That's neither here nor there," Zenas responds in a monotone, his eyes cast downward. "They're out, and I will have this done before I go home tonight. If you would please excuse me, I have a lot to do before I can start the lockdown. Thank you," Zenas says as he pushes the cart down the hall and around a corner.

"Poor guy has been trying to catch her eye from the day he got here, only to have the great doctor steal it. And now to have Nic get there to pick her up in her broken state," Mr. Risk comments as the two of them start walking down the hall together, away from Zenas.

"You know that I haven't been with Logan for years. It ended months before we started to see each other," Carol starts to explain in a panic.

Mr. Risk puts one finger on her lips and whispers, "His loss has always been my gain." He kisses her and begins to lead her down the hallway again. "So they are shutting down that lab? Are they shutting down that program, too? I thought the CEO would close down everything else other than that one. It's not like he has much time left to make his mark on this planet," Mr. Risk continues as if he's having a conversation with himself.

"Have you seen him lately? The last person I talked with who had seen him said he finally looked sick—but that was months ago. It was just around the time he made the announcement to the company about the creation of this new project and told us how every asset was to be available to the new venture." Pausing for a moment to consider the timeline, Carol continues, "Well, it wasn't really the *creation* of the project; it was just impossible for it to be kept secret any longer."

Mr. Risk slows to a stop, saying softly and with a far-off look, "I wonder if I can get on it now ..."

"Why would you want to do something like that? That is just asking for something bad to happen to you," Carol scolds, extremely concerned.

He starts walking again and responds, "They have been working on this program for a while, and no one knows what they are really doing. Do you? No, you are in charge of accounting, and they won't tell you anything." He concludes dismissively, "Besides, who says that something bad would happen?"

"Well ..." She begins by drawing a long breath. "First, there were just the lab accidents that happened with the 'chemical spills.' Did you hear that William's wife left him because of what happened to him? And two others died from exposure, and then there were a couple of others hurt in some kind of construction incident. Now two nurses and Dr. Rea have been murdered. The project is as cursed as the holy land of Green Glass," she says, with a seriousness bordering on fearful reverence.

"I forgot about the others," Mr. Risk pushes past the negative, "but I just want to do something more, and this could be an opportunity. I have been trying to get on this project from the start, but Logan blocked me. I almost quit the Green Sun Candy Company before they started this project."

"Well, it is a big company. You could have done something different, maybe something to get out from under Dr. Rea's influence." She fishes around for possibilities, "I know he had nothing to do with the candy arm of this company. I mean, he came from Red Inc. What would he know about candy?" Carol finds this conversation is becoming vexing, as she tries to improve her lover's darkening mood.

"Candy? Yes, because creating new, tantalizing flavors of candy is going to be a satisfactory use of my absurd skills," Mr. Risk answers sarcastically.

Carol looks at him sternly. "I'm serious, Carl," she says. "You can be such an ass sometimes." She then quickens her pace until she is half a step ahead of him.

As she rounds the corner, Carl says, "Oh, don't walk away mad!"

Almost to the door of the manager's office, she turns to him again and says, "I am not mad. We'll talk about this later; I've got to turn this report in."

"Carol, get your fucking ass in here!" booms a voice from the office.

"Shit!" she says under her breath.

"Wait!" Carl cries, attempting to detain her. Suddenly, the door of the manager's office cracks open. The manager himself appears. He is a towering man, with a girth that nearly matches his gigantic height. His cheeks are normally puffy red, but when he is angry, his whole skull turns cherry.

"You can play doctor with Mr. Risk later! Now, get in here!" he roars. Carol hurries into the office, leaving Carl with an apologetic glance. The manager follows, slamming the door shut and muttering loudly of Carol's uselessness. The massive blob of humanity then moves his way to his chair and throws himself onto it. A spike, triggered by the force of his mass, launches up through his corpulent ass and protrudes slightly from his colossal stomach. Blood splatters across the desk and Carol's face.

"Nyaaaaaaaaaa!" she shrieks in the most ear-splitting pitch possible. But, as the manager was already dead, it didn't really matter.

Carl, on the other hand, comes bursting through the door.

Aly is examining the chair on all fours. Remmington would have bent down next to her, but she is still wearing the heavy uniform. Instead, she gives the crime scene technician a soft kick in the butt, and says "Bang."

Aly jumps. Remmington chuckles for a minute before getting down to business.

"Glad you could finally join the party," Aly says, flustered.

"You have any idea how hard it is to go to the bathroom in these damn things?" Remmington counters. "Now, what've we got?"

Aly rocks back and kneels. "Well, we have a pressure-triggered projectile," Aly begins, "He's stuck to the chair—I think. Ms. Tuttle already gave me her account." She then points to the doorway, where Carol, Carl, and driver are engaged in conversation regarding the crime scene. It is clear that all three can understand what Aly and Remmington are discussing, since Carol has stopped talking and is looking at them. "I believe the trigger mechanism for this weapon required great force, achieved when the victim threw himself into the chair. The spike is four centimeters in diameter and forty-five centimeters in length."

"What about the entry wound?" Remmington asks.

"The spike is lodged through the victim near the anus and is clearly protruding from there," Aly replies, making a gesture to the dead manager as if to say, "See for yourself."

"Did I hear you right? The asshole now has two assholes?" Carl calls out.

The corner office is bathed in red sunlight, subdued by the dark blue wall that seals off the office. The blue wallpaper meets the corners of the glass windows, which form the other two walls of the triangular room. Matching cabinets meet these corners with the blue wall. All along this singular enclosure of blue are scattered photos of Dr. Rea's accomplishments, events, and travels. In truth, the seemingly random placement of the photos correlates to notes from a symphony that Logan played as a child.

At the ninety-degree turn of the room sits a crescent-shaped desk, recently disturbed. In front of this desk sits a pair of ivory chairs; they are odd looking and oddly comfortable despite being made of an alloy. This comfort is derived from the fact that the chairs adjust to their occupants. However, Dr. Rea's black, synthetic leather chair, which normally sits behind the desk, is cavalierly tossed on its side.

"No wonder there aren't any clocks in the office," Nic mutters to himself as he opens the third drawer, which is filled with boxes of watches. Most of these are broken, as opposed to those in the first two drawers. They are not of the same quality as those he found in the first drawer. He continues his plundering, searching for M.E. cards or other valuables to take Beth out and, of course, the mythical key that he believes Rea had. After having worked on the project with the good doctor, Nic hypothesizes that Rea has interactive models stashed away somewhere, and that finding them in the absence of the doctor will give him a leg up in the company.

In the middle of his great hunt, the door to the office opens, and Zenas comes in. He sees his fellow intern rummaging through his late supervisor's desk. "What are you doing, Nic?" Zenas asks, full of suspicion.

Like a prairie dog, Nic stands straight up. He flattens his multicolored tie and smoothes out his lab coat. He gestures to the disarray on the desk, and replies, "I was just taking care of a few of the doctor's things. I was asked to retrieve them by ... um ..." he fumbles his words, unsure of what to say next. He feels Zenas's gaze upon him. Nic moves around the desk and leans on the edge of it, trying to buy some time. "By Beth," he says finally. "Beth left a few things in here, when she and Rea were ... you know," he says, making a lewd gesture with his hands. Zenas masks a look. Nic puts his hands down. "Anyways, man, she asked me to collect 'em for her, and now I've finished."

"Good. Then we—can get started on the lockdown," Zenas replies. He doesn't like hearing about Beth like that. In fact, he wants to take Nic's head, bash it into the desk, and tell him he's a fuckface. But not wanting Beth to hear about such an act, he refrains from expressing his inner thoughts. "I hope you're ready to start," he chooses to say instead.

"Ah, yeah ... About that," Nic replies, giving a small sigh, mostly of hidden joy and perverted pleasure. "Look, Beth kinda wants her things ASAP, you know what I'm saying?"

Nic dances around an ivory chair and moves toward the door. "And she's leaving early today, because she needs some time off."

"Oh ... well, aren't you coming back?" Zenas presses.

"Sadly, no. She wanted me to ... well, she wants to go out with me tonight," Nic says. Zenas stiffens, and Nic takes secret delight in seeing it. He maintains his apologetic stance. "I really dunno what to say, Zen. But, I guess ... I guess she really looks to me as a good friend, right? I mean, I know she looks to you as one!" Nic can't help himself; he feels he was born to torment people like *this*.

Zenas's look is pure envy and hatred, all rolled up into his frosty green eyes.

Nic continues his emotional sadism, "But I s'pose ... I s'pose she wanted me to comfort her this time, you know?" *And you gotta stay* here *while I make that girl cry for a new daddy!* Nic thinks as Zenas's gaze shifts to the floor. The two of them stand silent for a moment. "Zen?" Nic asks. He can't tell if his colleague is going to hit him or do nothing.

Zenas's anger grows. Thoughts of Beth are the only things keeping him from lashing out. Soon, those thoughts have Nic involved in them, and he almost loses his control.

"Zenas?" Nic asks a second time.

Zenas finally looks up. The anger has been controlled, and now he looks at his colleague with tired eyes. "Y-yes," he stammers. "Sorry. I was just thinking to myself. Um, I'm sorry—what did you ask?"

"I was wondering if you were ..."

"Yes, the lockdown. Well, it's against policy, but I suppose the higher-ups can let this one be overlooked. I'll—take care of things," Zenas says, his heart breaking.

"You sure, man?" Nic asks; inside he is rolling with laughter. *Dumbass! Didn't you ever hear of nice guys finishing last?*

Zenas looks at his colleague. "Yes, Nic. It'll be all right. I can handle this," he replies, meaning more than just the current situation. *It will be all right. Beth will soon see how silly it is to get involved with this fool. She must see this!* Zenas attempts to console himself.

"Well, okay ... G2, it's—" Nic says abruptly, looking at one of the watches swiped from Rea's desk, which reads 5:30. "Shit, brother, I gotta run. Beth's clocking out now, and she needs to leave right away. You sure that you ...?"

"Don't worry, Nic. I have this," Zenas replies, a tad more gruffly than he expected. Nic recoils a little from the harsh tone, but regains his composure.

"Well, have a good time," Zenas says out loud, his tone icy.

"Yeah. Be seeing you, Zen," Nic replies, giving a half smile. As he steps out of the room, he thinks smugly, *Sorry, fucker; this chick's mine!*

I hate you, Zenas thinks.

Zenas stands for a moment facing the setting sunlight. The cool purple of the passing clouds reinforces his emotional state, and the solitude of the abandoned office allows him to break down.

Nic and Beth find a seat in the red-walled restaurant, a small booth. He studies her features: curly brown hair, soft peach-colored lips, small nose, and gorgeous hazel eyes, with a hint of sadness in them. He continues scanning downward until his eyes reach her chest. *Damn, girl—you are something else,* he thinks.

With a small smile on her face, Beth looks up at him from the napkin in her lap that she is absentmindedly folding and unfolding. Nic grins; his appearance is that of a hyena.

The atmosphere of the room is soothing; the lights are dimmed. Nic knows this girl needs the warm, comforting ambiance, if he is going to get anywhere with her. Most of the seats are high-backed, soft black booths, with tables and chairs covering most of the mahogany wood floors in the center of the room. The two of them scan the menu.

"See anything you like?" he asks.

Beth is silent for a moment. She glances through the menu again and then closes her eyes, taking in a deep breath.

"Well," she begins cautiously, and Nic gives her a look. "I mean, it all looks good. But, Nic, how can you really afford any of this?" she questions as she lays her menu on the table and withdraws her hands back into her lap.

He feigns looking hurt. *Cut me some slack, honey. Your pal Rea is payin' for most of this.* "What? You think you're not worth a filet mignon?" he jokes.

Beth giggles a little, and replies, "No, it's not that. It's just, the Company isn't really paying us much. You know, since Logan ..." She trails off, her eyes settling down to the tablecloth.

Shit, can't let this get away from me, Nic thinks as he takes her hand and squeezes it gently. She looks at him, her hazel eyes beginning to water.

"I know it's been tough," he says, trying to pacify her. "Doc Rea was something else." *And by something else, I mean he was the biggest putz I've ever known! Well, then again, there is Zenas ...* He refocuses on his prey and continues trying to cheer her up, "But we've got to try and find some sort of peace, right? I think Doc R—Logan—would have wanted us to try to be positive, you know, like that one time that bacterium almost escaped?"

Beth giggles. "You had some of its feces on your face!" she says, referring to a ludicrous inside joke among the lab members. She begins to erupt in laughter, pure and sweet in tone. Nic now wears an abashed face, yet he is secretly pleased. *It's a good ploy to use this story to distract her from Rea's lingering memory. So long as she isn't crying. Can't stand that shit.*

"Yes, thanks for reminding me," he smiles playfully. They are both laughing now. After a moment they become quiet, and she is looking at him with a warm gaze. *This is a good sign.*

"Want some wine?" he asks. She nods, and Nic orders a 200-year-old bottle, keeping its age hidden from his date. He assures his date's glass that it will never be half empty.

G-squared! Extra *strong, that'll do.*

They leave the restaurant after three hours. It was incredibly expensive, almost unheard of, but with the M.E. cards Nic found in the deceased doctor's office, he was able to pay for most of it; the rest he left unpaid. Of course, by the time the restaurant found out, they were gone.

"Did you enjoy it? The meal, I mean," Nic asks as they stroll away.

She looks at Nic with semi-glazed orbs, "Oh yeah! That was ... good stuff. I'm warm. Nic, am I hot?" she slurs as she puts the back of her hand up against her head.

Clearly, she is unable to coherently form a proper sentence without serious concentration. Nic panics a little, thinking he has overdone it on the liquid lubrication. He quickly formulates a plan for what he should do next, so as to keep her at a proper balance of inebriation. Like a python, he takes his arms and wraps her in close.

"I've got a *brilliant* idea," he says in a seductive tone. "Why don't we go to a place that can match your hotness?"

Beth lets out a flattered giggle and nods her head in agreement.

The line at the Imp Club is its usual length, which works perfectly for Nic's plan. As soon as they get through the door, he is able to have a drink in hand. To try and converse in the club is nearly impossible, due to the owner wanting the volume cranked that night. The sweating, writhing mass of humanity seems to twitch like corpses being given electrical shocks at each pounding beat. Nic sees this opportunity and takes it, keeping Beth on the dance floor, and utilizing the sexual-bending dance style.

While performing an advanced sexual-bending technique, Nic observes that the good doctor's watch is capable of glowing in the dark, and he is able to see what time it is. Realizing he doesn't want Beth to expire before he has conquered her, he figures now is the best time to escort her home. He leads her off the dance floor and walks her to the interns' floor of the

Green Sun Candy Company apartments and straight to her domicile.

Beth, intoxicated by both alcohol and promiscuous dancing, invites Nic forcefully into her bedroom.

I am a GOD! Nic thinks.

As their throes of passion end, Nic dismounts and flops over to lie next to Beth. Their chests are heaving from the exertion.

From above them in the darkness, a singsong voice says, "Young love."

Dark figure drops down from the ceiling, wielding two daggers, driving them through the two lovers' abdomens and pinning them to their sex altar. Nic, in pure shock and panic, swings at dark figure, who quickly grasps his arm and spins a blade up into Nic's hand, securing it to the bed.

Through pain and fear, Beth cries, "What do you want?"

Dark figure leans in close, grasping the hilts of the blades piercing their stomachs. As dark figure twists and shatters the green blades into thousands of shards, a single word is uttered in response: "Scream."

As dark figure departs, the two lovers oblige. Beth lasts only a little longer than Nic. Dark figure opens the front door, to be greeted by an open hand rushing toward the apartment.

"Beth!" Zenas exclaims, surprised and hopeful to see the opening door.

Dark figure intercepts Zenas's left wrist with their right arm and snaps it with ease. Dark figure holds the wrist and steps in and smashes the left ankle with their right heel. Zenas's cries of resistance are not of pain—that message hasn't reached his brain yet—they are from the exertion of his attempts to reach Beth. Continuing the counterstrike, dark figure is able to dislocate the right knee by bringing up their leg. Now the pain arrives, and Zenas opens his mouth with a scream. Dark figure then catches Zenas as he crumples, grasping him by his jaw, and holds him up to examine his features. Gently they push Zenas, letting him fall on his back with a dull thud.

Immediately, dark figure leaps up, pressing their back upon the ceiling, using it as a platform to increase their velocity, as they drive both of their knees into Zenas's exposed chest, delivering a blow severe enough to result in a flailed chest. Dark figure slides their legs into a straddle position, as they look into Zenas's panic-stricken face. Zenas struggles unsuccessfully to take in a breath. Dark figure can see him mouthing the name of the one he loves. They bring their face within an inch of Zenas's ear.

"Zenas, you'll be with her soon enough," they say in a placid tone.

On the thirty-ninth floor of a shared corporate residence building, Cassius towers over the big man who sits uneasily upright, as a med-tech examines and treats him for the injuries sustained in the attack. The man keeps holding the sides of his head, which delays the med-tech's progress in the examination.

Impatiently, Cassius prods the med-tech, "How much longer is this going to be? I need to ask him some questions."

The injured man answers, "Go ahead and ask; I will do my best to answer. My head is still a little fuzzy." The man continues to hold his head. The med-tech just nods with approval as he continues to treat the man.

"Sir, what is your name and your relation to the victim?" Cassius asks.

Tears well up in the man's eyes, as he answers, "My name is Pallaton, Pallaton Klen. That is my wife in the other room and my daughter in the room down at the end of the hall."

"Your daughter? What daughter?" Cassius asks, looking around for whoever failed to give him this information when he arrived.

Pallaton looks up at Cassius, "Her room is the door on the left."

The med-tech speaks up, correcting the briefing he gave Cassius earlier, "Sorry, sir. She appeared to be physically fit, so we removed her from the building, along with others that could be transported immediately."

Pallaton tries to stand up on shaky legs. "My daughter is alive?"

Cassius reaches out to support the big man and says, "It would appear that she is, and you will be joined with her as soon as possible. But for right now, I need to ask you some more questions, and he needs to finish addressing your head wounds."

Submissively, yet very happily, Pallaton allows them to help him back to a sitting position and awaits the next question.

Moving forward, Cassius asks, "Mr. Klen, can you tell me what happened here?"

Pallaton looks Cassius straight in the eye. "I was coming home from the site. I'm a construction worker, see?" he begins. "I normally get home about this time of night, but we had finished about two hours early and couldn't do anymore work tonight. So they sent everyone home. I was expecting the lights to be off when I walked in, but the set of lights over the fireplace were dimly turned on," Pallaton gestures feebly and reaches back to soothe the growing pain in his head.

"Mr. Klen, where are the controls for those lights?" Cassius asks, looking over at the fireplace and the mantel.

Pointing to two different switches on opposite sides of the room, "There and there," Pallaton continues. "The lights can be controlled from either one. As I said, the lights were on, which I thought was odd, until I heard a door close." The injured man casts his eyes to the floor in recollection, "I thought it was my wife coming down the hall. So I sat right there," he points to a high-backed lounge chair, "and I started to remove my work boots." He points to his left foot, still booted, and then to the right boot haphazardly flung in a corner. Looking at the knocked-over lounge chair and broken table, Pallaton is quiet.

"Please continue, sir," Cassius encourages.

With water welling in his eyes again, Pallaton looks Cassius in the face, "The next part happened so fast I am not sure if I remember it correctly." He takes a deep breath, and his eyes quickly dart past Cassius and peer down the hall. "I was taking off my boot, listening to the person coming down the hall, when it hit me that it was not my wife or my daughter. They had a different way of walking about them. When I realized this, I stood up, and I was trying to look into the dark hallway, but my night sight was messed up by the lights over the fireplace. They came at me so fast—I never got a good look at them. They must have grabbed that floor lamp as they came out of the darkness. They spun and cracked me upside the head, knocking me out."

"That would be consistent with this injury on your head here," the med-tech comments.

Cassius interrupts before Pallaton can finish his account, "Please hold on one second, Mr. Klen." Cassius turns away from Pallaton and the med-tech to focus on the radio.

On the other end of the radio is driver, saying, "Cassius, what is the situation there? Remmie and I are still about ten minutes out."

"There aren't many interviews to conduct. It's looking like this place was hit hard. Most of the victims come from the thirty-seventh floor. They are still trying to figure out how to remove the toxin in the air without causing more deaths. Aly was lucky that when the elevator stopped and the doors opened they didn't rip a hole in the protective membrane used to contain the toxin to the thirty-seventh floor. We're lucky it was Aly, 'cause she knew better than to try and go past it without testing. She found a stairwell entrance with another membrane protecting the outside world, and she was able to discover the poison," Cassius quickly informs them.

"So, how many interviews are there to conduct?" Remmington asks.

Cassius turns to look at Pallaton. "As of right now, just the one I am in the middle of. You can listen in if you like."

"That might speed things up; we'll listen in until we get there," driver agrees.

"I am sorry for the interruption, Mr. Klen. I know you want to be done with this, so you can be reunited with your daughter. Where were you in your accounting—the floor lamp, was it?" Cassius prompts.

Pallaton nods his head and continues, "Yes, that is right. They came out, grabbed the floor lamp, and spun around, hitting me in the head. That sent me into the chair, toppling it back to break the table here." He moves his hands slowly through the actions of the event. "The next thing I can recall for sure is the med-tech here trying to wake me up." Turning to the med-tech, Pallaton asks, "How did my wife die? Was it painful? Did she suffer?" His inquiry comes almost as a whisper as he chokes back tears.

The med-tech screws his face up, unsure how to answer or even if he should. The med-tech is saved from answering when Aly enters the apartment and answers Pallaton's question in a matter-of-fact way, "No, it doesn't appear your wife suffered at all. She was found lying in bed with no sign of a struggle."

"So was she killed like the people on thirty-seven?" Pallaton asks the faces before him, still searching for clarity.

Aly continues, assuming the other two in the room don't know as much as she does at this point, "The people who died on thirty-seven died a most painful death. To be honest, I am surprised that your wife is in the condition that she is in."

"Aly," Cassius cuts in, "what are you doing here right now?" His stern facial expression snaps her back to reality.

"I'm sorry. I need to collect ... um, the evidence," Aly answers in realization that she may have said more than she should have.

Not being fooled by the investigator's dodgy linguistics,

Pallaton asks in a cold, dead tone, "You are talking about my wife's body, aren't you?"

"Um ... there is also the object the killer left behind, and I have to sweep for anything the—they—may have touched," Aly stammers. She quickly turns to extricate herself from the awkwardness and to avoid any more of Pallaton's questions.

"What object was left behind?" Remmington's voice asks from Cassius's headset.

"Good point. Aly, what object?" Cassius asks.

Aly turns in a daze, still embarrassed by her faux pas. "What did you just say?" she manages to ask.

"What object, Aly?" Cassius repeats, even slower than before.

"Well, the murderer had to touch the doors, um, possibly some of the bedding ... well, um, her clothing and jewelry—" Aly begins, speaking somewhat sluggishly.

"Aly! What did the scumbag leave *behind*?" Cassius says, now gently cupping her chin with his nonmetallic hand. This has the effect of calming Aly.

"Oh. Well, they left behind a unique dagger," she says lucidly. Cassius then lets go of her chin, and she continues. "The blade is made completely out of green glass, with a very ornate handle, and it has religious symbols on it."

Pallaton speaks up, "Was my wife killed with this dagger?"

"No, it appears the dagger was just placed next to her body," Aly replies, "with no blood on it. In fact, it was placed next to her in a fashion that made it look as if it were being ..." she pauses for a moment, "presented to her."

"What do you mean, 'presented'?" Cassius asks.

"I—I don't know. It just looks that way when you look at the scans of the room," Aly responds, somewhat confused. "Do you know how much that amount of unbroken green glass is worth?"

"I—I don't care about that! Look, I know you've got to take my wife's stuff from our room, but—" Pallaton vocalizes. "Do—do you think I can have my wife's necklace? For my daughter? It's an old family heirloom of hers."

"Well, sir, I need to—" Aly begins, but Cassius cuts her off.

"Aly, it's for his daughter! What's the big deal?" he demands.

"Well, if anything, I suspect it was the one thing that the killer touched," Aly fires back.

"Why is that?" both driver and Remmington shout in unison in Cassius's ear. The big man shakes his head with a bit of pain and a lot of annoyance. He repeats the question to Aly.

"That's because the necklace has the same religious markings as the knife," she replies. "But I promise, sir, we'll get it back to you as soon as we've finished examining it. I'm sorry that I can't be of more help."

Through the radio, Remmington has Cassius ask, "Sir, can you just tell us a little about your wife?"

"She didn't practice the religion, if that's what you're asking," Pallaton responds. "The necklace came from her great-great-grandparents."

"Well, sir, could you just tell us about your wife, not just her religious life? Start with—I don't know—who'd she work for? What'd she do?" Cassius asks of his own volition.

Pallaton looks directly at him, and his eyes fill with a tired look. "She was a security access manager. She made the badges for staff members at the Green Sun Candy Company," he says to Cassius.

"Did he just say 'Green Sun'?" driver's voice asks.

The security guards walk into their changing room for shift change and begin to disperse to their private lockers.

"Hey, anyone seen the new guy? I thought he had finished his round and was going to be the first down here," the new guy's trainer, James, asks the general populace of guards.

"Did you lose another one again?" the former new guy, Marco, ribs.

James answers, "Hey, I didn't lose you. I ditched your ass. You smelled." James throws his used undershirt at Marco, hitting him in the back of the head.

Temper sparked, Marco aggressively returns the sweat-covered undershirt and tries to smother the much larger James. Holding Marco's arm back at the wrist that held the undershirt and fighting for control over the remaining arm, James takes a step into Marco and forces Marco's center of balance out of line, knocking him into a fall. James holds Marco's one wrist, and, while plucking the undershirt from the wrist, he says, "Now remember, little man!" James leaves it at that, clearly protecting some private conversation he has shared with Marco.

This doesn't have a calming effect, and Marco begins to scramble to his feet, as one of the other guards yells out,

"Oy! Who the hell blocked the shower-room door? I can't get it open."

James flicks a non-existent left ring finger in Marco's face, as if to say "don't mess with me," and then turns to join the rest of the guards, who are making their way over to the shower room. Message received by Marco, he remains seated on the floor. The frosted window is darkened, making it impossible to see what is preventing the door from opening. The guard in front is pushing on the door, unable to knock free the obstruction.

James places a hand on the man. "Hold on. I think the showers are running. Maybe the new guy is just playing a joke. Here." James begins knocking on the door. There is no answer or response of any kind, just the sound of water running. James then puts his ear to the door and listens, trying to find out who is inside and whether they are coming to open the door.

"That is weird; the showers don't sound right," James says aloud to no one in particular.

Back on the floor still, Marco calls out, "What does that mean? Get a light, you ogre, and see if you can tell what's in front of the door."

"Good idea, troll. Someone get me—thanks." James points the light into the shower room, revealing no more than a shadow or a line of something along the top of the window. Pointing the light at the bottom corner of door and door frame, James crouches to look for the blockage.

"What was that?" the first guard to the shower asks.

James stands up and looks into the shower room to see a human figure now outlined clearly on the other side of the door. The shadow drifts out of the doorway. James starts to pound on the door and door frame with both his hands in fists. When there is no response, he begins to become enraged and hits the door harder.

"James!" Marco suddenly yelps out but is silenced. James hits the door once more, causing the window to crack and a slow, undulating river of water to snake out from the crack. James turns to see what Marco wants, only to be met with the incongruity of seeing the front of Marco's bare chest, but the back of his head. Marco's head is turned completely in the wrong direction.

The water pressure turns the crack into a leak, spraying the back of James. He is unable to turn back to the door, as the window gives way to the water. When it shatters, the glass is followed by hundreds of gallons of water, forcing the big man to fall to his knees under the weight. The other guards are unable to stand as the water rushes past, taking them out at the ankles and causing most to fall flat on their faces.

James braces himself on all fours, until the body of the new guy flowing out of the window opening pushes him all the way to the floor. The water drains until the water line is equal to the bottom of the window line.

Half of James's face is submerged in the red-tinted water, as he starts to push the body off himself. Still running in the shower room, the water continues to flow, maintaining the window line level. The floor is slick, making it difficult to stand.

Recovering to all fours, James can hear splashing, and thinks, *What the hell? Get on your feet, guys. Quit splashing like a bunch of fish.* The splashing subsides, and the water becomes redder and redder. Looking up, James sees that all of his fellow security guards are bleeding out from critical cuts of the major arteries and veins.

Confused and shocked, James gets to his feet and realizes that all of them have expired. Still sitting upright with his head on backward is Marco. Standing on the bench behind Marco is dark figure, brandishing a curved blade in their left hand and staring into Marco's face. The point of the blade curves toward the ceiling so that the blood runs smoothly away from the point and pools at the hilt.

James doesn't move while looking at the bodies for a weapon. A couple of them have not changed, so they still have their sidearms. But all of the armed bodies are too far away to get to without alarming dark figure. James looks back at dark figure to see that they are still staring into Marco's face. Now they are flipping the blade, perhaps as a display to show how the weapon is well balanced, even though it is curved.

"I wouldn't," dark figure says in warning, without breaking their gaze.

This crazy fucker is trying to win a staring contest with a dead body, James thinks as he looks again at the closest weapon, which rests halfway out of its holster. *That'll increase my chance of getting the weapon out and getting a shot off before this fucker can react,* James strategizes.

The half-naked James dives for the weapon, acquiring it successfully, and pulls the trigger to hear a click. There is no round in the chamber. James does not panic; he efficiently chambers and fires a round at dark figure.

Hearing the click, dark figure remains motionless until the round is chambered. In a flurry of efficient motion, dark figure picks up Marco, using his body as a shield, and then, spinning off the bench, launches Marco headlong into James.

James fires three more rounds into Marco before they crash into each other. James drops the weapon and catches the force of Marco's body in order to stay upright. James holds Marco by one shoulder with his right hand and by a couple of ribs through a hole that the shots had made with his left hand.

Dark figure charges. James uses what he has as a shield. James lets go of Marco's shoulder and takes a well-placed swing, hitting dark figure in their left side. The blow does not faze dark figure, and in response, they cut into the Marco shield, whittling its mass down. James takes another swing, perceiving an opening, only to find empty space and receive a light cut across the back of his forearm.

Swearing at the sting and at himself, James uses the awkward meat shield as a club. Dark figure parries the club with their blade. James smiles as the blade slides between the ribs up to the hilt. James violently twists Marco's whole body, wrenching the blade free from dark figure's hand.

Surprised at James's strength, dark figure rounds a kick across James's open backside, pushing him up against the shower room door. James receives minor cuts from the leftover glass in the window frame. Then he quickly drops and rolls to his right, avoiding the following strike from dark figure.

James recovers from his roll, and now neither have weapons in their hands. Dark figure presses the attack with a left jab. James blocks the jab with his cut forearm, ignoring the extra pain that comes from having the cut struck. He dodges and blocks, retreating back and trying to find some dry ground. Dark figure doesn't tire as they continue to press James across the locker room expanse.

Finally, James finds himself running out of space to retreat. *The ground isn't dry here but is far better than in front of the shower room.*

James makes his stand. Deflecting dark figure's swing of the left arm, pushing it far enough to make an opening, James strikes dark figure in the same spot where he had hit them before. James tries to hit the same spot but finds nothing but air again.

The two circle each other, sizing each other up, looking for an opening. James feints and drops his guard with his right arm, creating an enticing opening for dark figure to strike. Dark figure takes the bait and swings with their left fist. James catches the punch and sticks dark figure in the side of the face. Dark figure reverses the grapple of the captured arm. Dark figure lifts James's arm, exposing his armpit, and plants their foot deep into James's ribcage just below the shoulder. The force of this kick, in addition to the pulling on the arm, causes a sickening, sucking pop as James's arm is dislocated. Adding to the injury, dark figure swings the limp arm like a tetherball around James's body.

James grunts from the pain and brings his good arm up to try to block whatever attack is next. The next attack doesn't come. Dark figure takes a couple steps back. James takes the opportunity and risks moving closer to the exit, keeping an eye on dark figure, especially to see if they are going for a weapon. Dark figure does not move to stop James, nor do they move to get a weapon to make it easier to finish James off quickly. Dark figure just moves in a line parallel to James.

The two stand staring at one another. Then, in an explosion of power dark figure charges. James is ready for this, and even with only one arm, he feels he can handle the onslaught. The world slows in James's vision as he readies for the impact. He takes note of the water splashing up and how dark figure is preparing for a left swing or a tackling charge, and he makes plans for both attacks. The moment before the collision occurs, dark figure dives feet first between James's legs, sliding on their back. They grab James's ankles, pulling him down. Dark figure lets go of James's right ankle and uses the left ankle to pull themself around, twisting his ankle until it snaps, as they stand up. From here dark figure steps on either side of James's left knee. They lock their legs around his, twisting and falling back down until James's knee and hip pop.

James's face is submerged, and the shallow water mutes his screams. He turns his head to the side and is able to take a breath of half water and half air. Dark figure is no longer entangled with him, and James doesn't know where dark figure has gone until a hand grabs his head.

"Go ahead and do it already!" James yells defiantly.

"I could have killed you at any point. You see this now. You fought well, and the fact that you are a Child of Pain makes me hesitant to kill you. That cult took your finger, and because they challenged me as God, I took your parents. It isn't your fault they fought God, so I bear no ill to you. In fact, many of your Brothers and Sisters of Pain have converted to my followers. I am tempted to offer you the same. So, what am I to do?" dark figure preaches.

James is in so much shock he has trouble understanding what is being offered to him. The water is now reaching James's lower lip. James says nothing as he coughs on the bloody water.

Dark figure flips James onto his back, bringing a fresh tsunami of pain, and then towers over him, saying, "I have to go finish something. You lie there, and if you are still alive when I get back, you can give me your answer."

Retrieving their blade and a uniform, dark figure walks out of the locker room, shutting off the lights as they leave. James lies shattered in the dark, feeling the water level rise.

Dark figure puts on the uniform and walks into the lobby to find only two guards sitting behind the desk. *Nice, no alarms yet. Well, let's see if we can change that,* they think to themself as they begin to move into position behind the first guard, who stands up.

"Crap!" the second guard exclaims, startled by dark figure looming over her companion's shoulder, just out of the first guard's reach.

The first guard spins around and says in surprise, *"G2!"* He is obviously unnerved by the encounter. "What are you doing here? The CEO has requested all security to his floor. Something has happened at the company residence."

"I know. Additionally, the guards from the last shift are dead in the locker room." Dark figure looks them both over and smiles beatifically. "All sorts of shit is fucked up now; you're kind of screwed," dark figure tells them.

"Wait—what? Who are you?" the first guard asks, as dark figure moves close between the two without elaboration. Their blade comes up under the protective plates of the standing guard, spilling his insides out. The female guard tries to pull her weapon and receives a backhand from dark figure, spinning her in her chair. She hits the alarm as she stops herself on the desk. Her partner has crumpled to the floor like a pile of dirty laundry.

"Thank you; that is what I wanted," dark figure says as they pull back the guard's head and slice her throat with the inside of the curved blade.

The silence of the lobby belies the terror that has just been unleashed. A single blinking light on the desk is the only indication that an alarm is screaming somewhere in the building. The only sounds around dark figure are droplets of blood falling on the desk and floor as the expired guard slumps in her chair.

A panicked voice comes over the deceased guards' radios: "All security personnel report to the CEO's floor immediately! This is not a drill!"

Dark figure runs for the lifts to see five guards piling into one of them. Increasing their speed, dark figure reaches the lift just as the doors are closing. Flicking their wrist, dark figure slips a curved blade past the closing doors into the guard in the middle of the group.

The doors close and the lift starts. As the lift rises, dark figure forces the safety doors open with their bare hands and jumps up to the underside of the lift. Dangling from the bottom, dark figure moves to a corner. Hanging with just their right arm, they pull out a straight blade and drive it upward into the floor of the lift. The blade strikes true, as is proven by the feel of the blade hitting more than just the flooring.

The guards stop the lift and begin to perforate the area around the blade in the floor. After a few seconds they stop; none of the guards makes a sound, waiting to see or hear whether the target is hit.

Over the radio comes, "What is going on in there? What are you shooting at?"

"Sir, we are under attack. One man is down and another is injured," a guard answers.

The voice on the radio answers back, "I can see that. How many are attacking?"

"Unclear, sir. I think we've taken care of this one," the guard reports with some trepidation.

"If they are taken out, then get up here and protect me," orders the CEO on the radio. "The guards in the lobby are already gone, and I can't reach anyone from the last shift to back you up."

The guard starts the lift again. As soon as the lift moves, the lights in the lift go out, but the lift still rises. Dark figure silently opens the top hatch to the lift, dropping down onto the dead body of the first guard. Dark figure grabs the weapon hands of two of the guards in opposite corners, pressing the firearms against the other two guards and dropping those two guards as soon as the shots enter their bodies. Pulling the arms toward the middle, dark figure aligns the firearms with the face of each remaining guard. Only one guard fires, shooting their counterpart in the face. Dark figure lets go of this fallen guard's arm. They then force the remaining guard's weapon back into his face, helping him pull the trigger as the weapon kisses the front of his neck, right above the sternum.

With the lights out in the lift, the CEO can't see who is alive or dead on the security feed. The CEO orders, "Open fire as soon as the lift stops."

From the darkness of the lift comes the chilly, sarcastic voice, "Because shooting God is a winning plan, you nihilist."

"Ignore them and fire!" the CEO barks in panic.

Dark figure taunts, "You fool—you don't belong and never will. I will cut you down to size, little man."

The lift stops, and before the doors open the remaining guards open fire. They fire until their weapons are empty. As the doors open, the air becomes heavy with the smell of copper and a mist of red from the bodies of the dead guards. Slowly the guards move closer to see if the attacker is finished.

Two guards wade into the soup of bodies. "I only count five bodies here. Whee—" is all one reports back, as the lift suddenly drops in a free fall. Hanging from the lift cable, dark figure shoots all the guards within the opening. The remaining guards down the hall return fire, ensuring their comrades in the opening do not survive.

The quick firefight ends as the guards once again have emptied their weapons. Slowly, the remaining guards move closer to investigate, reloading as they go. They open fire in the open space as they reach the killing zone where the first guards lie dead.

As the guards try to reload, dark figure opens another lift door to the guards' right and proceeds to open fire on the naked group of guards. Not a one is able to finish reloading before dark figure puts them down like rabid dogs.

"Do you see! Who do you think you are to challenge me?!" dark figure bellows in rhyme, down the hall toward the CEO's office.

"What do you want? I have money, weapons, drugs—anything. Just stop. I just want to live," the CEO pleads over the radio.

"I want none of those things, and you aren't looking just to live—you are looking to be more. Like a God, perhaps?" dark figure replies.

"More? What are you talking about?" the CEO asks incredulously, still panicked and puzzled.

Dark figure stalks down the long hallway and kicks in the office door as they riddle the CEO, "You don't know what it is to be me—the drug that I am, the drug I will be, the pure ecstasy. Here, let me cook up some of me!"

Dark figure kicks in the door. A shower of tempered glass greets them, as Driver crashes their vehicle backward into the office. Dark figure takes cover as Remmington jumps out and opens fire. Driver grabs the frantic CEO, who starts to struggle against this abduction. Remmington prevents dark figure from reentering the office, but driver knows that will not mean much if they don't get the CEO out quickly. Driver opens the back holding pods, and Remmington pauses her suppression fire to club the CEO with the butt of her weapon, knocking him out. Driver loads the body in the pod, pulls their sidearm, and adds to Remmington's fire. The two of them jump back into their vehicle and take off just as quickly as they had arrived.

Dark figure calmly stands up and walks into the office, watching their prize be whisked away. Losing sight of the vehicle, dark figure returns to the interior of the building.

"Sir, are you planning on doing 'business' on your busiest night?" Matt Levingston asks.

José leans against the rail, watching the news report flash across the screen in the silent Imp Club. He runs his knuckles over the scruff on his neck. "Yeah. I need to shave. How big's the crowd?" he asks.

"Twice as big as last year is what we guess," Matt answers.

"Well, isn't that a problem ...?" José speaks slowly, struggling to convey his thoughts to his security, unsure of how to explain what he feels. "Matt, we're going to have company tonight." He strides over to a chair, snaps his fingers, and beckons someone for a shave.

Bewildered, Matt says, "Isn't that the point of opening up tonight?"

"Well, Captain Obvious, it is, but those masses aren't who I'm talking about." José's sarcasm is not lost on Matt. "My friend will be showing up. I was hoping they'd have come before we open our doors. But, as you pointed out, we can't wait any longer." José leans back in his chair, awaiting his procedure.

Matt calls into his radio, requesting the security detail to report in.

"You know, Matt, this is my favorite holiday," José says to the guard, as he closes his eyes while he gets his shave. "You know why?" He doesn't wait for a response. "'Cause it's a joke! M.P. Day—we celebrate a guy who unifies everyone, so that people like me shouldn't be in business. Yet here we are, sitting in my club, with more Green Glass than anyone would want or need. And why? 'Cause I sell weapons!

"Music!" José calls out.

"Excuse me?" Matt says.

"Well, this *is* a club. We *do* have music, *right*? I think we should be greeting our guests with something that seems *fitting* for the hypocrisy of the holiday."

"Oh. Do you have something in mind, sir?" Matt inquires.

"Nah. Lemme see the playlist."

Handing José the playlist tablet, Matt asks, "Sir, do you have any instructions as to what we should do if your 'company' should show up in the middle of the party?"

José cocks his head to the side, looking at the guard. "Well, do you want to be burying bodies out in the desert tonight again?" The stunned look on Matt's face pleases José's sadistic side. "Then shut the fuck UP and stay out of the way! Let them go where they want. And before you ask, they *are* coming tonight. Just let everyone know," he orders.

"Sir, do you want to revise your private guest list for up here, since your—your friend is coming?" Matt asks nervously, reflecting on the response to his last inquiry.

José ignores the question and wonders aloud, "I wonder if they'll have my payment." Pondering, José then redirects the question to Matt, who is distracted by his earpiece. Annoyed by not having a response, José snaps, "Matt!"

"Sorry, José. The Residency just radioed in. Someone just showed up, asking where you were at and leaving you a very large package," Matt says.

"Ask, and receive! Payment is here, boys! Let's party!" José replies, raising his hands in the air with joy.

The crowd is thick as soon as José allows the club to open. The club is hot from the people on this unusually warm night, and José can no longer restrain himself from partaking in libation on his favorite holiday.

Upon ordering and receiving his third drink, José is surprised, not at seeing dark figure but at seeing dark figure serving him his drink. José accepts his glass and bows his head. "You want something to drink?" he asks dark figure.

"No, Mickey my boy, I think you know I'm here for other reasons beyond celebrating Mr. Parks's holiday," they reply.

The guests that José has been talking to stare dumbly at dark figure, confused by their words. "Who are you talking about?" one of the women asks José.

José ignores his guest's question and stands, waiting for dark figure to make their instructions known.

"Mickey, how rude! You have a young lady who is ignorant of this holiday's origin and its significance," dark figure says. Still baffled, José stands there, silent, mouth slightly agape, as he watches dark figure continue to engage the guests. "So, you don't know who Mr. Mark Parks is?" The young girl seems mystified by this peculiar person addressing her. They continue, "After all, it *is* M.P. Day, the day that celebrates the formation of the Global Council! But I would imagine it to be difficult for you to know Mr. Parks—or, as some of his friends, as well as his enemies, call him, 'Architect.'" Dark figure takes a sip of José's drink as if it is their own; José does not react.

"Architect?" the female guest asks.

"Yes, the great designer of your society," dark figure responds. "The birthplace and truth of all modern conspiracy theories."

"I'm sorry, I think you misunderstood me. I was asking, who is *Mickey*?" the girl says apologetically.

Upon hearing this, José snaps out of his stupor, "It's just a nickname that my friend here calls me by, and no one else." He is gruff and dismissive in his tone. "Now, if you'll excuse us, we have some business." He then steps between the girl and dark figure, motioning dark figure to lead the way to a seating area elsewhere on the third floor. As they sit down, the two of them order drinks.

Dark figure jumps right into business. "Your payment has been delivered, with a little extra for what I'm going to require you to do for me personally," they say. The hairs on the back of

José's neck stand. The dealer has physically done tasks for dark figure before, but never at their behest. Dark figure continues, "You know that I am here on a task. But to complete that task, I need to have some obstacles cleared out of my way. To do this, I will require you to 'betray' me."

The blood drains from José's face, and he drops his glass. He stands. José opens his mouth to protest, but dark figure quickly cuts him off. "Mickey, you won't really be betraying me," dark figure says soothingly. "It'll just look like you are to the rest of the world. Especially to the nonbelievers. Now sit down, order yourself another drink, and I will instruct you, so that you may deliver what I desire."

José complies with their demands, ordering two new drinks for himself.

"If you have not seen it on the news, Mickey, there has been an attempt on the life of the CEO at the Green Sun Candy Company." Dark figure smiles. "Now, while I may have missed the opportunity, my trip was not futile. You see, I was able to destroy those heretics' laboratories." The smile fades and sternness washes over the conversation.

"What I require from you now is to go tell the ones—who snaked the last thing I desire before I leave this city—where to find me. By this point, you are a person of interest to them, and it's only a matter of time before they drag you in and start questioning you about me. And you don't want *that*, do you? How would you explain the five-foot piece of Green Glass you have sitting in your front foyer?" Dark figure presents a smiling demeanor as they pause for this to sink in. "No, I think it's best that you go to them. Tell them I forced you to steal those things for the time I've spent here. Also, tell them that you are fearful that I will now be coming after you.

"You don't have to tell them much. All you have to do, Mickey, is tell them where I am," dark figure finishes.

"W-what if they don't believe me?" José stammers as he takes another drink.

"We'll get to that in a minute, Mickey. For now, you need to know where to send them," dark figure replies calmly. "I'll be at the abandoned warehouse of that company that was shut down for poisoning the CEO of Red Inc. What was its name again?" José begins to answer, but dark figure cuts him off abruptly, "Not important. That's where I'll be. Do you know where that place is, Mickey?" José nods his head, confident that even if he had forgotten the location of the place, he would make sure to find it. "Did you enjoy your evening, Mickey?" dark figure asks.

Absentmindedly, José replies, "Yes, this is my favorite holiday."

"Well then, you should call Matt over," dark figure replies while driving a green blade into José's side, missing all critical organs and breaking the blade off cleanly.

"There!" dark figure says with pleasure, as José looks up, grunting in pain. "That should be their proof that I will kill you. Matt!" they call for the guard, gesturing to the panic-stricken José with open palm. "You best get Mickey, my friend, to where he needs to be—and if he should die, I'm coming to kill you."

The whole way over to Civil Central Command, José and Matt argue whether they should be traveling there or to a medical center. They continue to squabble as they enter the Plain Room of the Command complex.

"I got this, Matt!" José yells, irritated. "I gotta do this! This has to be done first! It's not that bad, it's—aw, crap!" he complains as the blood gushes around his hand, which is holding his knife wound.

A different, but equally plain, greeter activates the security defense grid as the two men approach her. The now-transparent walls and ceiling reveal the hardware trained on them. The receptionist calls out the obligatory warning, "Do not move! State your business." Both men halt.

"My business *is* information, so that I can get this—" José begins, and lifts his hand off his wound, causing blood to splatter across his hand and onto the floor—"taken care of."

The man in the gunner turret calls out to them over the intercom, "There's someone on their way down to pick you up, Mr. Palmer." The room then fades back to its plain façade.

"Can we move now?" Matt asks loudly. The greeter waves them forward and stands there quietly, as José's bleeding lessens. The door behind the greeter soon opens and reveals a very tall man. The Cap lets out a sigh.

"Mr. Palmer, *why* are you bleeding all over this nice woman's floor?" he asks. "You know what? Doesn't matter." Waving off his question, he approaches the bleeding and distressed José. "I've been looking to talk to you anyways. Have you scanned them, my dear?" He shifts his attention to the young woman. She looks up at the plain ceiling, waiting for her partner in the gunner seat to report the information to her.

"Sir, they are clean," she finally confirms.

"And it's a good thing you are!" Cap says. "Otherwise, I

would've had them shoot you. This way, *gentlemen.*" The Cap wastes no time starting the interrogation as they traverse through the building. "So why are you here, José?"

"I've information about the mass murders," José replies.

"You *do?*" the Cap asks mockingly. "What kind of information?"

"The kind that can get you killed!" José declares vehemently.

"Then you better get it out quickly, before you bleed to death," Cap responds, unimpressed with the theatrics. They reach a lift and the Cap stands back, holding the door for his two guests. He escorts them to the forty-fourth floor, the medical sector.

Cassius hits the door twice, with a force that bends the steel core far enough to shatter the wood covering and expose itself. Following the second strike, Cassius takes two steps past the doorway before Remmington enters next, to cover the right, and driver follows to cover the left. These two steps are needed for both of them to get in through the door fast enough, so that a second later they can call their quadrants clear one by one. After it is clear, they move two more steps, giving Ben enough space to come in and back them up. They move together as a unit, without saying anything other than the word "clear" each time a new pathway opens up and nothing is found.

They have not moved far into the building, when Cassius stops moving forward. His silver arm unexpectedly drops to his side, releasing his weapon and slamming into his normal leg, giving him a charley horse. He doesn't make a sound but he winces in fear as he tries to take a step with his silver leg, which stubbornly remains still. He is trying to move his normal leg when very soft whimpering starts behind him. All of them have stopped moving at this point. Driver and Remmington have been spreading out to cover their quadrants, and they now turn toward Cassius and Ben to see why they have stopped. They also investigate whether a shot caused Cassius to drop his weapon on the ground when his arm fell. It is now apparent that Ben is the one crying softly. He isn't looking at anyone in particular; it is as if he isn't looking at all. Driver signs to Remmington to fall in, so that they can find out what is going on. Remmington acknowledges with a sign of "okay," and they both fall back to center around Cassius and Ben, covering their own backs. They reach Cassius at the same time, keeping their backs to him in order to cover him.

Remmington is anxious and asks in a stressed tone, "What's going on?"

"Dammit! My limbs—they aren't movin'," he replies with frustration in his voice.

"Okay, okay; do you think we could get you to some cover?" driver questions, scanning the perimeter for a defensible position to retreat.

Cassius jokes, "Dunno—without juice in these things, I weigh a ton."

Remmington tries to call out on her radio to get some backup, but she gets nothing at all—not even static. Her radio acts as if it has no power in its battery. Ben clears his throat. So driver falls back to a position between Ben and Cassius, in order to talk with Ben and yet still cover the left flank.

Driver asks, "Ben, are you all right?"

"If my lights going out is all right, then I couldn't be better,"

Ben carps in response. At this time, Remmington falls back to driver's position, still covering the right side.

"Maybe the three of us can drag Cassius back to the door. It's not that far," Remmington says optimistically.

"Lights out!" Ben responds in a little bit of a panic.

Driver responds by placing Ben's left arm on their right shoulder, guiding Ben closer to Cassius, and reassures him, "All you have to do is walk straight back, and all of us can help guide you out."

"All right, we have a plan!" Cassius says.

Remmington moves around to the front and slings Cassius's dropped weapon across her torso, giving him her secondary weapon, a hand pistol, as a replacement. Driver and Ben are standing behind Cassius, at the ready to help move him back toward the door. Ben is still holding driver's right shoulder, when a crack and flash of light from an elevated place in front of them hits Cassius in his silver arm, shredding it almost all the way off just below the shoulder. Remmington spins and opens fire before the second shot hits Cassius's silver leg, leaving nothing below the mid-thigh. Simultaneously, driver and Ben dive out of the way of the flying metal parts. Ben flattens himself as close to the floor as possible, as driver rolls into shooting position and returns fire. Cassius has fallen backward and lands in a sitting position, giving him the ability to open fire as well. Cassius has no pain, because his flesh is unscathed by the two shots. He is lighter, and this inspires him to think that as long as he isn't hit with another shot, he might cheat death again.

With the volley of shots from three weapons aimed at them, dark figure leaves the rifle where it lies and crawls back onto the catwalk. Dark figure is pleasantly surprised with how quickly and accurately this group responds to their aggressive help. Dark figure smiles, while rounding a corner that gives enough cover so they can stand up and make their exit.

Remmington sees that once the shooter gains cover there will be no telling where they go, so she bolts after them, yelling back to the other three, "Get out now, while you can!" With Ben still grasping driver, the two of them are behind Cassius before Remmington is done giving the order.

"Go back her up," Cassius pleads to driver. "With my leg and arm gone, Ben should be able to get me out, and I've got the eyes for him," he urges.

"She will need the help more than we will. GO!" Ben agrees, placing his right hand on Cassius and helping him up.

Driver takes the spent weapon from Cassius and trades it for their own. Running after Remmington, driver reloads the weapon.

Dark figure assumes that they will not split up to come after them. *No, they will help their wounded first and then come after me. That is their way.*

However, dark figure underestimates the group's dedication to their mission as a bullet whizzes past their head and ricochets off a few pipes. They turn to see Remmington, running with her arm straight out and firing her last few rounds. The shots barely miss, but only because she is running, and in response, dark figure dives through the nearest doorway.

Quickly springing to their feet, dark figure finds an ambush site and coils into position.

It is a very short wait.

Remmington breaches the room. Dark figure springs across the doorway and belts her across the face. Remmington spins as she is hit, and she collides with the floor. She lands sprawled on her back, with Cassius's rifle underneath her, propping her shoulders off the floor. Continuing their momentum, dark figure runs up the wall, flips, and lands with precision on Remmington's shoulders. A gut-wrenching crack fills the room, followed by murderous screams of pain, and then silence.

A wicked grin pierces dark figure's face as they have a private thought and then walk off.

Before dark figure can exit the area, driver enters to find Remmington on the floor. Seeing dark figure, driver raises their pistol to open fire, only to have it jam. They drop the pistol and pull out their secondary, loaded with a single tracking round and nothing more. Driver fires the round, and it finds its target in dark figure's arm. Driver starts to give pursuit, when they hear labored breathing coming from Remmington. Driver stays, giving up the chase for the moment, knowing that it can wait, and gives medical attention until medics arrive.

After they are found and Remmington is being cared for by professionals, driver makes their way back to the front, where Aly is already processing the scene.

"Come with me," she says, pulling driver by the arm.

"I need to go with my partner," driver protests.

"No! You need to see *this*," Aly responds and tugs them back into the building. Aly leads the way to a catwalk, where a S.Hi.T rifle and a tablet sit.

Annoyed, driver asks, "What do I need to see here?"

"This!" Aly says enthusiastically as she picks up the tablet, which displays two recordings simultaneously. On the left, the display shows the backs of driver, Cassius, and Remmington before they enter the building, while on the right is the view from the scope of the rifle. As the recordings play, it becomes apparent that the left side is what Ben has seen.

"This is the weird part," Aly says, pointing to the right screen. It shows that the rifle was perfectly trained on Cassius's silver limbs each time it was fired." A bewildered expression flashes across driver's face as they turn to Aly.

"This is why you needed to see this. There was no attempt to target soft tissue," she explains as she draws driver's attention to the weapon itself. "The rifle's fully loaded, which could've taken all of you out with ease."

The tomb-like darkness is interrupted by the faint glow of a small monitor lighting up the tiny room and the clicking of the ancient keyboard. Well below the bowels of the City, driver works at a backdoor node of the mainframe network of all computer systems, which gives them access to each and every computer linked into the mainframe. Even computers protected by the most robust levels of security, firewalls, and encryptions are laid bare to driver.

Driver's review of Green Sun Candy Company personnel files expands into scouring the private trade and inventory reports of a variety of companies and compiling different news articles about technologies related to the trades. Strange events begin linking together, forming a complex web in driver's mind, when the tracing beacon embedded into the perpetrator comes back online with a single beep.

Driver stops researching and holds their breath, waiting to see if what they heard is real or a phantom of exhaustion. After ten seconds, the beacon beeps again. They pick up the tracing indication interface and bolt for the surface and toward the City. With every meter closer to the surface and the waning light of the sun, the signal becomes stronger. By the time driver reaches the vehicle, the attenuation of the signal from all the material between driver and the surface has been eliminated, and the signal is strong enough to give them a direction of southeast to travel and an estimate of the distance. The beacon is well outside of the City operational boundary.

The signal was masked and only now shows up. They kicked the crap out of me and out of my team. Yep—it's a trap.

Climbing into the vehicle, driver loads the tracing indication interface into the vehicle's computer system. Heading toward the signal, they simultaneously work on removing the kill switch control so that they can travel outside of the operational boundary. By the time the boundary warning shows up on the front screen—WARNING! THIS VEHICLE WILL

NOT OPERATE OUTSIDE OF THE CITY LIMITS. TURN BACK NOW, OR THE VEHICLE'S OPERATIONS WILL SHUT DOWN!—driver has removed all outside influence on the vehicle, giving them full control of weapons systems and the freedom to travel outside of the boundary. They increase their speed as they cross the boundary. The recently vacant front screen now displays an ominous warning: UNKNOWN THREAT, which quickly reclassifies UNKNOWN as MISSILE.

"G2," driver curses, attempting to jockey the vehicle out of a collision course. They are almost successful in this maneuver, but the lethality of the missile is discovered when it splits apart, revealing it to be a Spydertech missile.

"G2!" driver curses aloud once more.

Realization hits driver like a sledgehammer; they know that, at this range, escape is nigh impossible, and their demise is at hand. Yet, in this dark situation, a beacon of sunlight reflects off the fuselage of a missile failing to maintain the synergy of lethality. Driver observes this with some relief, as the missile vacates the upper left quadrant. They know this is the only chance of an escape. They take this chance and direct the vehicle through the opening. A wave of relief begins to pass over them, when a new volley of missiles appears, causing relief to turn back to dread. This time the missiles come from the rear and below. The onslaught forces driver to take the vehicle to a higher velocity and altitude with the intent to outrun.

As each missile runs out of propellant and self-detonates, driver only feels one of the concussive blasts. A small rain of shrapnel rakes the vehicle. With a deep breath, driver takes stock of the tracking beacon. Noting both the deviation from the required course and the lack of new missile threats, driver redirects the vehicle southward to intercept the beacon.

Frustrated by these attempts on their life, driver pushes the vehicle to its limits, which, according to the vehicle manual, is ill-advised. To add to their vexation, another Spydertech materializes. This third assault is from the front, only slightly to the right of driver's vehicle.

As the missile deploys into multiple warheads and draws near—far too close for driver's comfort—another one of the warheads strays off course. An opening to the left forms after this errant missile veers and detonates, taking out another projectile. Driver makes a hard left and steers the vehicle through this hole, just barely clearing the wave of missiles. Off-course again, driver arcs the vehicle in a roll to the right, correcting the bearings. This maneuver orients the vehicle to the west. Driver throttles back and begins decreasing altitude in a long, smooth glide.

Close to the horizon, the sun blazes brilliantly, obscuring driver's vision. While their sight contains dancing orange orbs, the missile warning comes on again. Unable to determine the display before them, due to the sun's brilliance, driver is dragooned into crashing the vehicle, threading between all of the missiles.

The vehicle inflicts more damage to the ancient pathway, shadowed by the skeletons of timeworn towers, than it sustains. As the dust settles, assisted by the breeze whistling through the rusted metal bones, driver can make out the darkened silhouette of the figure standing on top of these fallen bones.

"Like these buildings, which have not stood as long as me, so you shall crumble and be washed away," the figure calls down in a calm, confident, and condescending tone. Turning on their heels, they walk down the back of the building they are standing on, out of driver's sight. Over the ridge of the building, driver hears the figure's inflammatory echo, "When this is all done, I will donate your shoulder blades to your partner."

The mere mention of their hospitalized partner, as well as being shot at multiple times with missiles, pushes driver to their breaking point. They rush up to the apex of the decrepit building, hoping to catch the figure. Suddenly, driver halts short of the peak. Despite being overcome with rage, driver has the clarity to discern that they have no idea what awaits them on the other side. Driver reaches into the belt of their heavy armor and pulls out a flash grenade. Pulling the pin, they throw it in the direction in which the figure disappeared. A bright flare ignites, and when it has settled, driver pulls their service pistol and rushes over.

The figure marches right back up the side after driver has thrown the flash grenade, surprising driver as they both reach the top at the same time. The figure, faster than driver and easily able to sight them, grapples with driver's weapon arm. The figure steps into driver and flips them over, away from their crashed vehicle and toward the figure's original direction of travel.

Driver lands on their back, cushioned by the sand and rusty flakes that have accumulated over time. It is all around them, but it does not hold them where they fell. Driver slides down the back side of the building, picking up speed due to the near frictionless surface of their armor. Sliding feet-first down the embankment, driver digs their right heel into the loose sand, anchoring themself enough to spin around quickly. As they are about to open fire on the figure, driver crashes into a wall and slides down a sandy stairwell, losing their weapon in the process.

Driver can see the opening they came through shrink in size

and is only slowed twice by the landings in the stairs on the way down. Once at the bottom of the stairwell, driver slides another forty feet before coming to a stop.

In the dark, driver lies on their back, cursing to themself about what just happened and trying to figure out where they are. There is only enough light to see the openings like the one they just came down. With the distances between the lights, driver estimates that there could be almost a block between openings. Driver kicks their legs over their head and does a backward somersault to come upright with one knee on the ground still.

Yep, a subway. Well, at least it doesn't smell like one, driver thinks as they look around for the figure. In the dark subway, driver's eyes slowly adjust until they can make out where the tracks are. Driver realizes they had almost rolled over backward into the track pit. The pit is inky black, so dark that the bottom cannot be seen. The drop should have been only three feet or so, but driver is unsure.

As driver moves away from the edge and back toward the light from the nearby stairwell, there is a loud crash to the driver's right. Preparing for an attack, driver turns toward the sound and sees light emanating from the floor.

Cautious, driver walks over to the edge of a hole three meters in diameter. Dust obscures the view through the hole, but it is clear that something is moving at the bottom. Something about the size of a person.

A piece of rebar launches up from the bottom of the hole and just misses driver's face; it harmlessly embeds into the ceiling of the subway. Driver reaches for their last two stun grenades and finds one missing. *One is better than none,* driver thinks as they pull the pin and drop it down the hole. The concussion from the blast causes the hole to crumble and widen, forcing driver to back up and lose sight of the figure, as more dust fills the air between them.

Driver searches for a stairway that will bring them down to the unknown level that the figure had fallen to in the middle of their failed charge. At the end of the platform, driver finds a set of stairs that plunges into unknown labyrinthine tunnels. The evidence of steel gates has almost completely rusted away. Only two bars on one side and three on the other side of the double doorway are left. Driver slides through without contact, yet two bars on the one side fall to the ground, landing with a soft clanging as a dust cloud of rust erupts.

The descent is nineteen stairs, and somehow it is even darker at the bottom. Driver is able to place their fingertips on each wall while standing in the middle of the passageway. The walls have breaks in the smooth surface about every fourteen inches, at irregular intervals when comparing one hand to the other. It isn't long before driver finds another passageway. Driver's fingers fall away from the walls as they stop in the crossing of two paths. The new passageway runs perpendicular to the current path. Driver reaches out in front of them to see if the current path continues. Their hands smack into a door that nearly falls off its hinges when they touch it.

Driver steps forward and stumbles through the doorway, as they miss the first step down in the black. The handrail maintains its tenuous hold on the wall long enough for driver to regain their stance across two different steps, facing back up the way they had come. Driver hugs the wall to their left and turns around to face down the stairs. Situated, driver reaches out for the opposing wall and finds their hand touches nothing. Moving their arm around, driver realizes that they have found a hole in the wall. Driver submerges the arm deeper in the hole to find it is shallow and that there is something inside. The object is loose and is easily removed from the hole. Running their fingers over it, Driver receives a blinding light to the face as their thumb inadvertently presses the switch to the Nova Beam flashlight.

Torch in hand and pointing the right direction, driver is able to move much quicker. These stairs and this passageway are much smaller than the first set but longer. At the bottom, driver finds themself in the middle of a crossroads, with seven ways to travel. Eight, counting the stairs. The paths are not of the same size nor are the walls down the paths made from the same material. About half look as if they have been cut by hand; they also look newer. On the floor, driver can see a random letter in front of each path, including the stairs, where they stand on top of the letter *L*. *The letters are definitely the last thing added to this place.* Each is cut away and stenciled in a different font.

"D, I, L, M, N, O, S, and T. Which way to go?" driver says aloud. Cave-ins make it easy to eliminate the paths marked M, T, and I. None of the three paths goes more than twenty feet before the cave-ins are reached. Path *D* is missing its floor and has no visible way around or down. Turning around, driver tries the pathway marked *N*.

The *N* path is not a straight path. It meanders, with a slight downward slope to it. Driver notes that there is a bundle of cables running along the ceiling and recalls seeing similar bundling before in the other tunnels and one other type of place. Traveling down the path for a bit, driver estimates they have reached somewhere near the depth that the figure had fallen to. Turning a sharp corner, driver can see light around the next corner. Extinguishing the torch, driver moves as quickly and quietly as they can in the heavy armored uniform. The closer driver gets to the opening, the more information their senses can tell them about what lies beyond in the light. First there are the sounds of electricity humming and moving metal parts. Then the smell and heat. The smell is a mix of different chemicals and has a tangy taste.

The makeshift path does not open up into a huge factory or large open area, but into a well-lit and -kept hallway, with white walls and fluorescent lighting. *Not at all what I expected.* To the right, the hallway continues down for a while to other passages, and a door can be seen at the end. Immediately to the left is a pair of double doors with broken-out windows, from which the smells, heat, and noise emanate to assault driver's senses.

On the floor in front of the doors lies the broken glass from the windows; it's mixed with tacky blood. There is a trail of splatter that is easy to see against the white hallway. *This is quite the obvious trail of bread crumbs. I wonder where the neon "trap" sign is.* In intersections there is more blood, making it clear which way to go, and during long stretches there is no blood until another intersection is reached.

The path that driver follows twists and turns at every intersection, until the path comes to a doorway that looks strangely familiar, like one of the many doors driver has to pass through to get to their node beneath the bowels of the City. This door looks to be of heavy steel, with the section of wall around the door being steel, as well. In the top steel sill of the door, "dnimtsol" is gouged into the steel. Bloody handprints on the door handle encourage driver to pry the door open enough to fit through.

Driver crosses the threshold of the door. Lying in wait, the figure throws a reverse roundhouse kick to driver's left side. Prepared for the ambush, driver catches the kick and redirects the power and momentum to slam the figure's backside into the steel door casing.

The impact causes driver to let go of the figure's leg. Driver presses their counterattack with a right jab, connecting with the figure's left chest. Then driver throws a left hook. The figure dodges by falling into a roll to their right side.

The roll places the figure up against the wall. Kicking off the wall, the figure shoots back and tackles driver in the abdomen. Rolling over the top of driver, the figure removes two pieces of the protective armor. One piece is the right under side, and the other is the left shoulder. Continuing, the figure uses their momentum to stop in a standing position.

The figure stomps at the center of driver's chest, but driver rolls clear before the heel of the figure can connect with anything other than the ground. Driver rolls four times to try to create enough space to get up. Driver is able to push themself onto all fours, when the figure charges, kicking driver in the side. The body armor absorbs most of the impact.

Driver uses the force of the kick and pushes themself to their feet. Standing ready, the two face off. They begin to rotate in a clockwise direction, looking for an opening in each other's guard. Driver has their hands up by their face in fists, while the figure has their hands open and covering about mid-chest height.

Driver swings with their left and then right. The figure dodges the first swing and redirects the second to go harmlessly wide. Driver is able to bring the first arm back in time to cover, leaving no opening for the figure to counter.

Down the path the two continue, once again looking for the opening in the other's guard. The figure swings a couple of test jabs. Driver pulls back to dodge them. Driver aims a roundhouse kick low to the figure's right knee. The figure lifts their leg, taking the kick in the shin. As the figure steps down, they reach out and grab the left underside plate, pulling driver's unprotected right side into the figure's left knee while removing the armor plate.

Driver gasps, winded, but they remain standing and back away. The figure throws down the armor plate they have retrieved and steps closer to deliver a side kick. Driver reacts instinctively and grabs the figure's foot with both hands. Driver holds the figure's foot and then pushes back in the opposite direction with their full force. With only the one leg beneath them, the figure falls backward and lands prone.

Not recovered fully yet, driver backs up more instead of continuing. The figure kicks up on to their feet to see driver more than twenty feet away and moving back even farther. Sprinting to close the distance, the figure takes two steps on the wall, transitioning into a flying kick. Driver dives into a somersault headfirst toward the figure, kicking their right leg up and catching the figure in midflight with the backside of driver's leg and heel. This not only forces the figure to stop their direction of travel but reverses the figure's trajectory. Finishing the forward roll, driver slams their right leg down, with the figure attached.

The force of the figure hitting the floor creates a spiderweb of cracks. Driver sits up and folds their legs, ending up sitting on their knees on top of the figure. With a left-right combo, driver starts to knock the figure's head back and forth. The figure twists their head just enough to dodge the second swing from the left hand, causing driver to strike the ground. The pain from this missed strike is clear on driver's face, as they grab the figure by the hair with their left hand. Driver lifts the figure's head up to line it up for punches from their right arm.

Crack. The figure slams their left knee into driver's back, breaking a smaller back armor plate and sending driver tumbling over the figure's head.

The two rise slowly, each obviously in pain and tired from battle, facing each other once again. The figure spits out a mouthful of blood and pulls their hair out of their face, while driver reaches back and removes the broken armor plate that is stabbing them in the back.

Both fully recover; they try to assess how much fight is left in their opponent. Their eyes meet. Controlled fury in driver's eyes meets the cold, calculating darkness in dark figure's eyes—eyes that can pierce the soul and that will leave a person shattered. They are Death's eyes.

Suddenly, dark figure drops their stance and stands upright, quiet for a moment. Driver almost lets their guard down, letting their arms drop a fraction of an inch, but then brings them right back up. Dark figure stands silent and lets a sadistic grin appear on their lips. They turn on their heels and walk a little way down the hall into another room to their right.

The door is unlike the other doors in this hallway. It has a resemblance to the crossways with the lettering on the floor. It is not part of the original layout of the facility. Driver cautiously looks and assesses that it is a circular, empty room. The walls are covered with mismatched steel panels; they have pipes of a similar style as the panels running in every direction along the walls.

Driver rolls their head, cracking their neck, and gets ready for the ambush that they are sure is to come as soon as they cross into the room. *Not a neon sign, but close enough.* Driver walks willingly into the trap. Nothing happens. The room is not just a circle with about a fifty-foot diameter but a cylinder that rises all the way to the surface, nearly two hundred feet. For some inexplicable reason, it has been remodeled, but driver can tell that this was once a missile silo.

There is an echo of metal grinding against metal. Driver spins to find dark figure hanging from a pipe right above the door, about twenty feet off the ground. Dark figure still holds the same smile as before they walked away. The pipe dark figure hangs by slides an inch and echoes once more. Dark figure does a pull-up and drops their weight on the pipe again, but still hangs in the air. After the second time, the pipe comes free, and dark figure lands on the ground, with a good-size pipe about the size of a *bo* staff. Dark figure looks back at the doorway and, for the first time, looks disappointed and frustrated.

Driver quickly follows the line of pipe that had not broken off. It connects to a makeshift portcullis that failed to lower. Dark figure intends to trap the two of them in this room.

Displeased with this prospect, driver does the only thing they can do and charges the now-armed dark figure. The charge surprises dark figure, and they are slow to stop driver from grabbing the end of the pipe. They nearly break the pipe with the opposing forces applied; it is sent spinning out of both of their hands. Driver throws a right hook but is forced to block dark figure's double-sided attack toward driver's head. Driver blocks both arms at dark figure's wrists, keeping their arms wide. Dark figure drops their head and slams a headbutt into driver's upper sternum. Driver stumbles back three steps.

Dark figure closes the distance and throws a right hook. Driver blocks with their left arm and counterstrikes with the heel of an open right palm into dark figure's throat, nearly crushing dark figure's windpipe. In the same counterstrike, driver slips their right leg behind dark figure's leg and presses even harder, forcing them to fall to the ground.

Driver continues to the doorway and turns to see dark figure holding themself up with the pipe they were once hanging from. Wheezing, dark figure stands upright and hurls the pipe at driver, missing by a hair. The pipe embeds in the wall, piercing a bundle of wires. Driver pulls the pipe from the wall.

Red lights start flashing and horns blare. A soothing female voice broadcasts throughout: "Perimeter breach. Facility destruction immanent. Four kilometers is the minimal distance required to be free of the blast."

"More like *fourteen,*" dark figure laughs with a raspy voice. Driver uses the pipe to trip the gate mechanism to close it, as they turn and run back out into the hallway, trapping dark figure who had planned this for them both. Driver only looks back to see that the gate has closed fully and then runs as fast as they can back to the surface.

The disembodied voice continues to call out her warning without emotion. Driver knows there is not much time and they have a long way to go.

On reaching the intersection with the letters, driver hears the same female voice start a countdown: "Two minutes." Impeded by nothing, driver makes it to their vehicle with twenty-one seconds left on the countdown. The takeoff is rough. Driver counts in their head, *ten, nine, eight, seven ...* Driver's countdown is interrupted as the ground explodes and the fireball engulfs the vehicle. In less than two seconds, driver finally escapes the fireball and reaches a truly safe distance.

Missiles, crashes, fire, and explosions have taken a toll on the vehicle, forcing driver to stop. Driver gets out to see the vehicle smoking but not on fire. Shaking their head in amazement, they turn to see the old city ablaze. Driver takes a deep breath, only to choke on the smell of burned flesh. Driver checks themself to see if they have been burned. The smell comes from the back of the vehicle. Driver peels away the body part that the heat melted there. The orientation of the hand and the thumb clearly identify the arm as the right. Driver examines the severed arm and notices that the underside of the arm near where the shoulder should be, which laid up against the vehicle, is unburned.

Driver looks closely at the undamaged flesh and drops the arm in shock as they see the light-blue numbers tattooed there.

Remmington's vision is blurry, and she is not sure at first who is standing at the foot of her bed. *Bed? This isn't my bed, nor my place,* Remmington thinks to herself. "That's right, my arms," she groans in whispers, as some dull pain makes it past the drugs and she tries to adjust herself so she can see who is there.

The windows are covered and the door is closed, so the person by her bedside is a darkened form. Only a little light from outside of the room, mostly from the outside city lighting, makes its way in.

It becomes clear that it is her partner, as they begin to speak while they replace her medical tablet. "I'm sorry this happened to you," gesturing to her broken shoulders, "and I am sorry even more for what still must happen to you." The voice is familiar but cold. "But before that, you will be rewarded for your pain and suffering with knowledge unlike any."

It will soon be finished, driver thinks to themself. The large lobby with the dome roof is an impressive place, inlaid with the company logo of the Green Sun Candy Company. Driver is the only non-security personnel in the lobby as they wait.

The contrast—from the abundant surface light to the darkness, where their eyes strain in the faint emanations from the backdoor network node monitor—is uncomfortable to driver. The irony to them is that the light of knowledge is gained here, in this dark place.

These words of apology kindle a small panic in Remmington, tempered only by the pain returning in her arms as she tries unsuccessfully to rub her eyes to help them focus more. A squeak of a word escapes her, "What?"

"Here," driver says, as they help her with a drink of water. Standing closer, they are no longer blurry. Remmington can see the damage and some of the pain that her partner has endured, but she is unsure of when or how. Remmington wonders, *Did this happen at the warehouse? Maybe sometime after I passed out.* Her private pondering is clear on her face.

"This didn't happen at the warehouse. I found them, and I have put an end to it all." Driver pauses, giving this time to sink in. "There is a lot more than you know, and I want to tell you. Please don't interrupt me," driver gently pats Remington's hand, "because you might hurt yourself, and I must tell you everything quickly."

Quickly—why quickly? Remington thinks. Her involuntary groans indicate she is in no mood for dialog anyway; she is perfectly content to just listen. *I do hurt, so it's not like I want to say much anyway.*

"I know why they attacked and killed so many of the employees of the Green Sun Candy Company. They had a goal, and they almost completed it," driver tells her while offering another little drink of water.

"Damn you, Architect! G2—I hope you are rotting, wherever you are!" driver curses, pushing themself back from the screen and dropping their head into their hands. Frustration is mounting, as driver searches for the key to understand how any of this is possible, let alone why they had been left in the dark about this revelation.

Sitting up abruptly, driver resolves to redouble their efforts— when they pause to reflect on something they saw.

The lift chimes as it reaches the lobby. Three guards, armed to the teeth, step out. They block the line of sight of driver, but driver knows who is behind them. It is the person they wait for and the same person a few people outside are waiting for, as well.

The unit of three men has two more fall in to cover the flank of their package. The group walks to the middle of the lobby where they meet with driver.

"Oh, how nice it is to see you again. Can you help me out of this mess?" the CEO asks with a warm smile from in between the guards standing in front of him. "Am I in danger again from the person who attacked me in my office?" the CEO quickly asks as the smile disappears from his face with the thought of that attack.

Driver looks around the lobby, notes the spacing of the other security personnel, and asks cordially, "Can these men move away so that we may talk privately?"

"Their goal is not really understandable without knowing some history," driver tells Remmington as they start their narrative. "Now, this history goes back to before the formation of the Global Union, the tragic event of Green Glass and the religious group linked to that event; it goes back to when antiques were nothing more than new items for sale. The time before year one E.E."

"Okay, go and check to see if we are clear for my vehicle to come pick us up," the CEO barks at his guards. He then informs driver, "You have until then to say what you came here to say." As he finishes, he pulls a small inhaler out and takes three quick hits, looking dejectedly at driver.

Driver takes a second to assess what causes the quick change in the CEO's demeanor. Not wholly confident of the reason, driver asks an easy question. "How long do you have until your sickness fully consumes you?"

The CEO's mood changes again when he displays an arrogant smile. "Recently there have been some tragic setbacks, but I think I will be the first one in my bloodline to beat my sickness."

"So, why do you think these setbacks occurred?" driver asks, confident of the answer.

"The setbacks? You are asking me the cause of the setbacks? You know the cause," the CEO responds exactly as driver has anticipated. "A complete lack of protection by you and your department, and failure of leadership by your superior." The executive points his finger literally at driver, "That is the cause of the setbacks. I've been searching my employee records, trying to find others that can replace the ones that you have failed to protect. As soon as this mess outside is resolved, they will be briefed into the project, and then they can complete it."

The callousness and quick reaction that the CEO takes to the mass murders of his employees is not completely surprising to driver. Driver asks, "What do you think is the cause of the disturbance outside right now?"

"It was the end of the era A.D., and the planet population was moving exponentially toward fifteen billion people. I know schools teach that this is just a theory, but it's a fact. There were many different governments: a couple of good ones, but most were terrible. None were perfect. The failings of the different governments aren't really important for you to understand what's happening here in this time. What is important is that these governments fought a lot with one another, in many different ways. Sometimes it was financially or politically, and sometimes there were physical wars. The latter caused them to focus on the surface of the planet and not the real danger to their government and their lives," driver tells Remmington as she sits quietly, looking puzzled and trying to understand why this history lesson is related to her being in this bed. Her eyelids flutter as a wave of pain stabs through her.

Driver logs out of the node and waits for the sign-in screen to refresh itself. Taking a deep breath, driver thinks, *I hope I'm not making a mistake by doing this.* The node only asks for a log-in. Driver types D, N, I, M, T, S, O, L. The screen becomes dark, snuffing out the only light in the dark room.

"Crap," driver says.

After a loud series of metal-on-metal clanging of doors locking, the screen comes back alive.

This is not an authorized node for you, Lost Mind. Are you Lost Mind? These words light the room from the monitor.

Confident that lying at this point would be a bad idea, driver answers by typing "no."

Seeing how you are not this log-in, you will be asked some questions. Failure to answer satisfactorily will result in your demise. Do you understand?

Driver enters, "Yes."

Are you an operative?

"Yes."

"Those few people outside are upset because the stock for Green Sun Candy Company is falling, which is acceptable right now because of the panic caused by the murders in the apartments. This drop is not a representation of the strength of the company," the CEO declares. "People think this company is going to be left with no workers and have no future if we have to replace all of the talent lost with inexperienced personnel. So I've started a campaign to purchase back stock. This way, once the project is resumed and then completed, the Green Sun Candy Company will be the richest company and possibly the most powerful." A tight smile flickers across his face. "Just a little inside knowledge for you to maybe … increase your position," the CEO shares, acting as if he has just given driver a great gift.

Driver smiles politely, "And what if the Green Sun Candy Company doesn't finish this project before your sickness finishes you?"

Disturbed by driver's continued questioning, the CEO's tone becomes edgy. "As I told you before, I will be the first of my family to beat this sickness. I don't understand why you are taking such an interest in this project."

"Because this project is tied to things *you* don't understand," driver responds with the first hint of force.

Remmington's thoughts drift back to the first part of what her partner has said, about rewarding her with knowledge. She hopes the puzzling history lesson isn't the reward for her pain, as it shoots across her shoulders again for no reason. She winces with the pain, fearing that moving or even breathing will cause it to increase in severity. While distracted by the pain, she misses part of whatever driver is explaining.

Something about superpower countries, I think? Whatever they are. I hope I didn't need to know that, she humors herself after the pain subsides again.

"Well, once a few of the superpowers had discovered this imminent global disaster, they embarked on some pretty strange and erratic behaviors, which drew attention from other nations. These lesser governments tried to understand the strange behaviors the superpowers were displaying. The tipping point was the mind-blowing amount spent in purchasing raw equipment and the huge amounts of land that these countries were putting aside. They even took steps to protect the secret from being discovered—breaking treaties and destroying satellites that could have spied over the areas that were under very strict quarantines. Another clue was that the superpowers no long tried to stop world hunger or world atrocities, like genocide. It took some time, but all of the large and powerful countries eventually learned why the superpowers were acting so irresponsibly to their populations and to smaller allies. By this point, many countries had taken over land to procure the raw material they needed. Some had switched from democracies or republics to police states, in an attempt to make it easier to control the population. It didn't really matter; the planet had less than six months," driver states in a tone of indifference.

Driver's tone has the desired effect, and the CEO takes a step back and starts to look for his closest protection detail.

Driver takes a nonthreatening half step back from the CEO, inviting him, with palms out, to come back to the middle of the lobby floor. "You are about to run out of friends. I will be the very last one you have." Driver folds their hands in front of themself, like a patient parent waiting for an unruly child to calm down. "So please, come back over here," driver says, gesturing to the ground in front of them.

Cautiously, the CEO recovers the ground he just retreated from. "So, why are you my last friend? That doesn't matter much anyway—I will just buy friends once we complete the project," he says. Driver raises an eyebrow at the CEO and then looks back at the dark mass of a mob that has now gathered outside the lobby.

Please identify yourself, operative, the screen asks.

"the hated," driver enters in.

Operative the hated, do you know the whereabouts of operative Lost Mind?

This is the line of questioning driver has feared. Driver hopes that identifying themself will unlock the system and doors. Driver knows that the nodes are protected from people trying to use the system, and now with the doors locked by the system, they understand why human skeletons are occasionally found at some nodes. The system locks anyone in for answering questions incorrectly. Incorrect answers are predetermined by the software program developed by Architect.

"Yes," driver answers. Driver hopes that this is satisfactory to the software, and by extension, to the designer, Architect.

Were you given the operative's identity by freewill or torture?

Driver knows why Architect asks this question; in fact, this question is a direct response to when driver gained the new operative name "the hated" and their current *mission.* Driver at one point had skillfully obtained the identities of different operatives and used them as they saw fit. Clearly this was before Architect had implemented this version of the program.

Extrapolating the time frame for when this program was developed, driver confidently answers, "Neither."

You have just given a response that must be explained further. Explain.

"Lost Mind failed to protect a node that they were assigned to," driver types in, sitting back and holding their breath, with the hope that they had not given Architect too much credit in programming the system to understand such an answer.

Turning back to the CEO, driver answers, "As strange as this might seem to you, I am less confident that you will have as much success buying friends as you are leading yourself to believe."

"Well, unless you are going to tell me that my attacker is going to kill me, I have no reason to believe that my confidence is false," the CEO says smugly.

Driver says, "No, I have already taken care of the attacker and have seen to the loose ends myself."

To the best of your knowledge/understanding, where is Lost Mind at this moment in time?

Hoping that the truth will be acceptable, driver enters, "Most likely dead."

What proof do you have that they are deceased?

"I have their right arm. It was removed from them by the force of an explosion."

Were any other body parts recovered?

"No."

At what coordinates or location did this explosion occur?

"Southeast of this node, within five hundred kilometers." Driver absently adds, "Just over the node that Lost Mind failed to protect."

After typing this in, driver exclaims to themself, "Crap, I might have just screwed myself!"

There is no response or new question for a couple of minutes, leaving driver in the dark, literally. Eventually the screen posts: *Your answers to the next questions are vital to your survival. Was Lost Mind's latest mission completed to satisfaction before the destruction of that node?*

Driver cannot fathom all the details of dark figure's mission, and with no other choice but to give some answer, driver gambles, "Unable to answer."

Unable for fear or for other reasons?

Thinking, *Yep, this was definitely written by Architect, that bastard,* driver types in: "Reason of unknown parameters of Lost Mind's mission."

The screen goes black.

"The technology was severely lacking for what was needed to save everyone. So the only solution was to try to save the human race as a species, not in totality. Seeing that the planet wasn't going to be viable, spaceships were built," driver explains.

Remmington coughs upon hearing this and thinks, *Okay, I did miss something important.*

Driver looks her over and can see that the ramifications of what they are saying are finally sinking in. "Remmie, are you okay? Do you need any more water?" driver asks.

Remmington gently shakes her head no.

"Okay, I will continue, then. The problem wasn't building ships big enough to house people and resources for long periods of time. The problem was that the ships couldn't travel fast enough to get to another planet that was suitable for sustaining life," driver explains dispassionately.

Unsure of how much she's missed, Remmington finally speaks

again. "Wait, why did they have to leave? But we are still *on* the earth." *These must be really good drugs.*

"What loose ends?" the CEO asks incredulously.

Driver answers factually and without emotion, "You don't belong. Your company went about buying a number of failed companies that were destroyed by massive numbers of deaths, and usually fire,—collecting them in order to start this project that you think will save you. But as I said, you don't belong."

A chill runs down the back of the CEO's neck when driver says this again. As he peers into driver's eyes for a long second, recognition and hope dawn in the CEO's eyes. Leaning in, the CEO asks, "So it can be done, then? You have seen it work?"

Driver nods, adding, "It has been done, but it can never be allowed to be repeated." Driver checks the growing crowd outside. "This is why your employees were murdered and why all of those companies you bought were decimated and had to shut down." Looking back at the CEO, driver continues, "If you hadn't been so focused on the possible life-saving properties of the treatment, you would have seen the pattern in the downfall of the remnants of the companies you were gobbling up."

"*Pattern?* You really think I didn't see the pattern? I just thought, since the last company was destroyed so long ago, nothing would be in my way, and I would have a shot at saving my life." He feels justified in his logic. "And if what you're telling me is true, that the attacker or murderer has been taken care of, I will be able to save my life. That's all the loose ends, right? ... Unless you are going to kill me now," the CEO adds, once again nervous about the possible danger that could come from driver.

"I don't want to kill you, nor do I *need* to kill you. Your sickness will do that. Well, that is, if the mob doesn't get in here first," driver says, pointing over their left shoulder to the growing masses outside the windows.

Driver moves closer to Remmington, looking over her IV drip and making sure it is working correctly. "It looks like you are getting the right amount of medicine." Remmington smiles faintly.

"The earth was going to get hit by a true planet-killing asteroid." Driver returns to the narrative. "This wouldn't just wipe out life on the planet, it would split the planet into pieces. The superpowers tried to destroy it or break it apart, with plans akin to the stuff of movies. Mostly what they accomplished was to fire hundreds of nuclear warheads at it before they realized they couldn't break it apart or move it far enough out of the collision course."

Astonished, Remmington no longer registers the pain from her arms. She is about to ask driver something when they continue, "Remmie, I will tell you how the planet survived as best I can. But I don't fully understand all of the science behind how we are still standing on this rock. The key things to know are: we *are* still standing, and what happened all that time ago is why the world is the way it is now." This all seems cryptic to Remington, so she lies quietly and tries to stay focused on the major points of this saga unfolding before her.

"So the planet was going to be destroyed, and no other home planet was reachable within one lifetime for the spaceships that were being built. Secretly and quietly, the superpowers started to launch ships into space, first trying to set up bases on the moons of this solar system or the planet Mars. This effort was limited and was not a long-term solution, and it was agreed that this would still be the extinction of the human race. But humans are stubborn creatures. They had tried to set up five of these colonies before they had finished the first long-distance space traveling ship. They hoped these ships would be large enough to carry enough people and supplies for a few generations, so that humanity could make it to planets that they hoped would be new earths. The first two ships left on the same day and were sent in opposite directions for their long journeys. Amazingly, the superpowers were still able to keep these launches quiet somehow. Before they were ready to launch the next ships, one of the superpowers found a man with the solution that would allow people to live long enough so that there would be only one new generation or perhaps the original generation making it to the new earths."

Sitting in the dark, driver contemplates if there may be another way out of this tiny room. They start to move on their hands and knees, looking for some kind of opening to escape through. *No, I can't get out of this vent—it is just a three-inch pipe. I don't even know if this is a vent. I don't feel any air flowing from it.* As with most thought processes, these are riddled with both enlightenment and doubt. *It is too high on the wall to be a drain pipe; besides, that is under the chair. And nope, that is no bigger. I wonder if this is how the other bodies died down here—by attrition.* The density of the darkness weighs heavily on their eyes, almost to the point of being painful, as the eyes try to acquire light—any light.

Feeling the edge of the one and only door in the dark, driver all of a sudden sees that the room is once again lit by the green glow from the node.

On the screen is: *Please stop crawling all over the floor. You will now be briefed on Lost Mind's mission, and then you will take over and complete their mission to satisfaction. Do you understand?*

"Yes," driver enters as they sit back in the chair.

Lost Mind was given free range to do as they pleased, as long as they fulfilled one constant mission. Their mission directive: the Methuselah treatment must never be allowed to be repeated.

Driver asks, "What kind of free range?"

Lost Mind operated and moved without fear of ever being cataloged by any computer system. Their DNA, fingerprints, and face, if ever captured, cause a specialty program hidden deep within the network to run, which scrubs the system that makes the identification. This is possible because all government and private computer systems are linked. Records show that Lost Mind was flagged not too long ago and required a blackout to cover up the scrubbing.

The current target is the Green Sun Candy Company. Lost Mind believed the CEO of the company is dying from a genetic disorder. Last report filed by Lost Mind states all employees and physical evidence of the Green Sun Candy Company's work on their new version of the Methuselah treatment has been purged.

Special operational note states they believed they had to remove the local law enforcement due to their dedication to protect. Lost Mind was given authority to use extreme prejudice if needed to remove the obstacle of the law enforcement. Lost Mind ended the note with an addendum saying that was not necessary.

At this time, the only mission threat is the CEO of the Green Sun Candy Company. The hated, you will finish Lost Mind's mission and take it over from now on.

"Will I be given the same freedom as Lost Mind, or will I be contained still?"

Containment has been lifted, and your current mission is ended, as well.

The sounds of deadbolts drawing back echo through the darkness.

You will also no longer be the operative 'the hated'; your new operative ID will be Balance.

The mob outside, as if on cue, starts to beat on the windows, causing a crack to form, as driver drops their arm after pointing them out to the CEO. The security guards don't move and are focusing on the words coming through their earpieces.

"What is going on?" the CEO asks, panic rising in his voice.

Driver calmly answers, "Remember, I am your only friend right now. You no longer have any money or even a company to run. The Green Sun Candy Company has just fired everyone, and all of its assets are gone—due to a 'computer error.'" Driver walks behind the executive while continuing to explain. "Those people out there have lost everything, and your name is attached to the reason they have nothing." Driver leans into the man's ear from behind, just to make sure he attends to the words, and continues, with a hint of amusement in their voice, "I think they want your blood." The CEO stiffens. Driver continues to walk around the CEO until they are in front of him, facing the crowd outside. "This 'computer error' first transferred all the employees' personal assets to you, and then you lost all the assets, but they don't know that part. They just know you have all of their credits." Driver turns to face the CEO. "Oh, and just to make it interesting, you have sent a letter to them all stating that you don't think very much of them."

Wide-eyed and with dropped jaw, the CEO looks at driver. "How could this be done?"

"*I* did this to your company, so that your project will *never* be completed and to ensure you'll have no credibility to ever restart it," driver answers in a cold, level tone. Folding their hands together, they wait for a reaction from the CEO.

"You? How are you my friend, if you've done this to me?" the CEO demands, outraged, looking very nervously around the room and noting the security guards' growing confusion.

Driver takes a deep breath and suggests, "Simple: you might be able to get away if you walk out that side door," driver looks toward the door but does not point, so as not to alert the guards or the howling mob to the proffered avenue of escape. "Get into the vehicle that's waiting for you, and drive yourself to another city before that glass breaks." Driver looks back at the pressing crowd again.

Still dumbfounded, the CEO stands there, looking back and forth from driver to the side door and then at the glass and back to driver. *Crash!* The massive glass windows of the lobby explode inward as the mob presses forward to achieve its desire. The CEO starts to run for the side door, yelling once again at driver, "How are you my friend?"

As the CEO reaches the side door, driver calls out loud enough to be audible over the mob, "I didn't just kill you."

The mob, with murder in its eyes, rushes past driver and the guards, who make no effort to intervene.

"The treatment was given to all the people who were selected to go on the remaining ships." Driver walks to the window. They look out at the city, at the lights pushing back the oppressive, dark night. Finding comfort in the darkness, driver feels that it is a good setting to share secrets, so they continue. "The treatment has had a couple of different names, but the effect is still the same. Those who were treated no longer aged or, well, didn't age as fast, depending on how well the treatment took." Driver stretches to release some of the fatigue of the recent battle. As they mindlessly watch others outside the room, an old phrase pops into their head: "Ignorance is bliss."

"At this point, we call ourselves Methuselahs." Driver turns to Remmington and waits for it to register.

Remmington fires off in rapid succession, "*You* have had this treatment? You are a Methuselah? How old are you?"

Driver smiles, "I told you that you would be rewarded with knowledge." Driver avoids a direct answer and decides to give Remington more information first. "The last ship that was going to leave before the planet was destroyed was compromised. The general public found out and destroyed the ship before we could board and launch." Driver walks back to Remington's bedside. "Consequently, a population of Methuselahs was stranded here on the planet for what was going to be the end."

Remmington interrupts with one burning question: "How old are you really?"

Driver looks away, avoiding eye contact, while trying to think of an answer that won't terrify her. "Older than I'd ever intended. And yet," driver begins, "not old enough to do all the things I thought I'd do ..." Their voice trails off as they inwardly contemplate this revelation. "Remmie, I could try to explain what my age is, but the significance of it will not be clear unless I share more of the hidden history with you first. Understand?"

Remington nods without a sound.

"The planet didn't end, because all of the nukes did more than anyone had known. The small trajectory deflection from the nukes positioned the two objects to ricochet like two pool balls that just barely touch one another, moving the earth's orbit and changing the length of a year. Not by much, mind you, but enough to make it look as if the planet were gone when the ships that had left tried to look back and see what had happened to their home. To add to this illusion of complete annihilation, the radiation from the nukes energized the higher atmosphere, so radio signals failed to permeate out from the surface or penetrate down from space. If the ships did discover it, the earth would have looked like a giant dead rock. The radiation was not enough to cause harm to the life that was able to survive the impact; there wasn't that much life, but it was enough to rebuild."

The two of them sit quietly until Remmington starts to ask

her question again. Driver preemptively answers, "I don't know how to tell you how old I am." Driver laughs. They know Remmington is not going to give up. "I can tell you I'm over seven hundred years old at this time." Remmington's mouth hangs agape in astonishment. "There were years—possibly decades—before people attempted to form a civilized society. As new governments were formed, the survivors inevitably tried to model the old ones. The quickest groups to gain power were religions." Driver begins to pace the room. "Confusingly, it was a group of secularists and atheists who collected leftover nuclear warheads and set them off in the holy lands of major religions. The intense heat from the warheads over the sand created the Green Glass Zone." Driver flings their arm toward the window to indicate someplace beyond the room. "The fanatical fear and hate of these secularists and atheists almost ended life on the planet for a second time." Driver looks down, away from Remmington, their thoughts recalling many things never to be shared with her. "Ironically, this also caused the formation of two more religions." Driver looks up. "One religion is the faith of Green Glass. The other religion, Pain, is faltering at this point, and the only remnants left in this society seem to be their children, or rather, the Children of Pain. The perpetrator we've been chasing was the leader and founder of the Green Glass religion; this lunatic survived hell on earth and walked out of the Zone after the attack, believing themselves to be a god."

"They are a Methuselah, too?" Remmington asks weakly.

"Unknown to me until just recently, yes. But they—we—all of us are not just Methuselahs. Seeing the pain from all the wars, we started to outlast governments and then started to run some governments ourselves, which only became an issue when the ruler didn't age. So this is how the current government was born. The remaining Methuselahs eventually became the keepers of balance and followed the one who developed the treatment. He was a very smart man, whom everyone knows and celebrates to this day," driver explains, testing to see if Remmington is still paying attention.

"Who? How?" Remmington whispers, becoming hoarse.

Driver smiles and offers Remmington more water. "M.P. Day is his work. He has held the highest office on the planet four times now, by changing his face each time. Then, after a while, he'd kill off that persona." Driver appears to be absently checking Remmington's IV drip. "The Council knows nothing about Methuselahs and believes *themselves* to be the ruling force of this government." Remmington struggles to keep her eyes open and remain conscious. "Leaving the Council to run the government, until it was needed for him to take over and readjust the system, is found to be the best way to maintain control. Maintaining control is why there are laws for almost everything, such as the birthing laws I helped write. The Council is like an autopilot for the government. Its existence allows us to move in and out of power without much notice. People don't realize it's the same person that becomes leader of the government time after time. They think they're getting someone new, but they're not. This is why there is sometimes no leader over the Council, like right now.

"I believe Mark Parks died while having his last face change. He was much older when he got the Methuselah treatment, and his body couldn't take any more abuse.

"As for abuse, your body has taken a fair share," driver continues. "For what I must do next, you shall not be conscious." Driver leans in close to her face and whispers, "This is the part for which I am truly sorry. I have changed your dosage, which will cause you to fall into a medically induced coma." Her pain is being pushed back into the darkness, and her mind follows. "You probably won't remember much of this," driver takes her hand and gently pats it, "but it's better that you don't get questioned about this—questions regarding what I'm about to do and the fact that I'm about to disappear.

"People will think that the history lesson I gave you is just a dream, which should keep you safe."

Remmington's eyes grow heavy, as she fights to stay awake, and she closes them for the last time. She tries to talk, but she is too weak and is slipping out of consciousness.

"I do hope you survive."

... Is the last thing she hears.

Driver explores what it truly means to have freedom in the network. From the node, they learn how each of their lives was generated and how the timing-clock program was set up to transmit new orders and a new life and identity to them at random intervals.

Relieved that their *mission* is over, driver thinks, *I alone can choose what I do with my life again. No more waiting for a new life to start and losing my connection to those I meet—the punishment is over.*

The last new thing driver finds with their freedom in the network is the flight roster for the ship they were supposed to be on before it was destroyed.

Inside the file is a list of serial numbers that coincide with the tattoos on their inner right arms. Driver recognizes their own immediately and then picks up the mutilated limb of dark figure and finds the matching number. Across from the serial numbers is a description, either ACTIVE, DEACTIVE, or UNKNOWN. There is one listed as UNKNOWN. Driver assumes this one is Architect, since they are unable to change its status. For the rest, all but three are listed as DEACTIVE. Driver engages the corresponding numbers from the severed arm and changes dark figure's status to DEACTIVE, leaving only two active members

The driver and one other.

ABOUT THE AUTHOR

Nicholas B. Beeson considers himself a storyteller, not a writer. Nicholas enjoys people's interactions and reactions to challenges; he draws on his degree in psychology and his experiences. After traveling the country during military service, he lives in Wisconsin with his cat. This debut novel comes from a decade-long dream.

Made in the USA
Lexington, KY
15 March 2013